Done to D

A MYSTERY-COMEDY
IN TWO ACTS

By Fred Carmichael

SAMUEL FRENCH, INC.
45 West 25th Street   NEW YORK 10010
7623 Sunset Boulevard HOLLYWOOD 90046
LONDON   TORONTO

STORY OF THE PLAY

"Sheer lunacy is probably too mild a term to describe Fred Carmichael's latest play . . . it is all for fun and the premiere audience responded enthusiastically to what must be the most improbable stage production imaginable. It is a rare moment when a laugh is not heard. . . . Mr. Carmichael's funniest play and his most original format. Ingeniously packed into the script is a parody of every mystery plot, hero, and villain created in the past fifty years. The story alternates between reality and imagination as five mystery writers wrestle with the problem of writing a television mystery series. All around them murders occur and each writer takes a turn at solving them in his own style. Surprise follows surprise and then Mr. Carmichael raids the box office for his last generous handful of laughs." (Glens Falls, N. Y., *Post Star* review of first Summer Theatre production.) Five once famous mystery writers; a couple who only write the most sophisticated of murders, a young author of the James Bond school, a retired writer of the hard-hitting method, and an aging Queen of the logical murder, involve the audience as they explore their own methods of investigation on a series of murders. Finally, a member of the house staff is murdered, and the laughter reaches its peak for the final curtain. Doubling of some minor roles is possible. ". . . took the audience for a very special roller coaster ride. . . . Mr. Carmichael plays a skillful and fast-paced game of guess again with the audience. . . . Mr. Carmichael's most clever and most rewarding." (Bennington, Vermont, *Banner*.)

DONE TO DEATH had its first performance at the Dorset Playhouse, Dorset, Vermont, produced by The Caravan Theatre, Inc., Summer Stock Company on August 5, 1970.

DONE TO DEATH

by Fred Carmichael

Staged by Patricia Carmichael

CAST

JESSICA OLIVE	*Elizabeth Franz*
WHITNEY OLIVE	*Charles Dickens*
MILDRED Z. MAXWELL	*Susan Loughran*
BRAD BENEDICT	*Alan Tongret*
RODNEY DUCKTON	*Fred Carmichael*
JASON SUMMERS	*Howard Enoch*
STAGEHAND	*John Charles*
JANE	*Hillary Maveety*
GREGORY	*Bruce Peyton*

and

Barry Baughman	*Roxane Lynn*
Jeffrey Doty	*Phyllis Restaino*
Jill Geiger	*Patt Schneider*

Set and lighting designed by Barry T. Baughman

ACT ONE

SCENE 1: *A television studio. Evening.*
SCENE 2: *Vulture's Vault—an island in the Caribbean.*

ACT TWO

A few minutes later.

5

DONE TO DEATH

CAST OF CHARACTERS

JESSICA OLIVE—an extremely attractive and sophisticated woman in her middle to late thirties. To her, everything is a joke with a reason to laugh. She and her husband are the epitome of the rich, devil-may-care type of characters who used to be so prevalent in mystery stories and they play their characters to the hilt. She wears an attractive and smart dress, carries a large tote bag, and a turban hides her hair for most of the show.

WHITNEY OLIVE—a few years older than JESSICA, he matches her in wit and sophistication. Always the perfect gentleman, he is dressed in the latest fashionable suit and might well have walked out of the pages of *Esquire*.

MILDRED Z. MAXWELL is a large woman, folksy in a way, but very determined and opinionated. She often has a sharp way of speaking, although she is a friendly soul. In her late fifties or early sixties, she wears a two-piece silk dress and a small hat.

BRAD BENEDICT—he is much younger than the others and, consequently, more mod in his dress, but by no means "hippie." Actually, he is a very shy and retiring person, quite the opposite from the characters he writes. He has a quiet sense of humor which manifests itself in a small grin when he has been amusing, but usually he takes a back seat and admires the others. He wears a bright tie, blazer, and slacks.

6

RODNEY DUCKTON—the oldest of the five authors, but he is extremely vital and constantly interested in everything that goes on. There develops a small rivalry between him and MILDRED and a small generation gap noticeable between him and BRAD. He is dressed impeccably in a suit and is always full of boundless energy and enthusiasm.

JASON SUMMERS—a man in his thirties, efficient-looking right down to his horn-rimmed glasses which he occasionally removes to emphasize a point. He wears a neat, Madison Avenue suit. He is enthusiastic about the project before him but terrified it will go wrong and he will lose his job; hence he has a nervous air about him, plus an always-eager-to-please-everyone attitude that makes him seem on the verge of collapse.

STAGEHAND—dressed in a work outfit of dungarees and denim shirt, he is unimpressed by anything that happens around him.

JANE—she is an eager, young, and pretty maid but one suspects, for a time, that her naivete is not all pure. She wears a blue or green maid's outfit with appropriate apron.

GREGORY—dressed in a typical formal butler's outfit with swallowtail coat. He somehow looks remarkably like a Dracula character with his dark, penetrating eyes and deep widow's peak hairline. When he speaks, it is in a deep, Middle-European accent.

GEORGE—is about thirty and dressed in a bright, pinstriped suit with the unmistakable wide lapels and shoulder padding of the thirties. He speaks in a very soft and sophisticated voice which almost purrs his villainy. A wide-brimmed hat covers most of his face and dark glasses cover his eyes. He has an overcoat over his shoulders and wears his left arm in a sling.

MAN—the same type wide-brimmed hat, sunglasses and overcoat as GEORGE. When he speaks, it is with a tough, staccato voice.

MARTHA—typical of the thirties movies, she is dressed in a stunning negligee and wears jewels on her neck and both wrists. Her hair is done in a severe style and she speaks with the voice of a hardened woman of the world.

GIRL—the epitome of the twenties ingenue. She wears a beaded dress of the era. Her eyes are widened to their fullest circle with pure innocence. Her hair is a mass of curls and when she moves it is in the manner of the early movies.

MONSTER—should look as horrible as possible. Possibly he wears one of those rubber "Frankenstein" masks and rubber claw-hands. He has a dark coat on and wears raised, thick-soled work shoes. When he moves it is a leaning forward walk to give the appearance he would fall over if he didn't walk.

STEPHANIE MILDAUR—a beautiful girl in her late teens. Although innocent, there is a certain worldliness about her which has come from her life surroundings. She wears an attractive dress and hair style of the forties.

SECRETARY—as modern as they come, she is dressed in a trench coat with bright boots. Under the coat she is wearing only a bikini. She speaks with a slight foreign accent and is breathtakingly beautiful.

BOX OFFICE GIRL—(or house usher) exactly as the audience sees her (or him) when they enter.

NOTE: Doubling of some of the roles is possible and is up to the discretion of the director.

8

Done to Death

ACT ONE

SCENE 1

A television studio. There is a set up which will remain throughout the play. It is the living room of Vulture's Vault, an old mansion on an island in the Caribbean. The room is very old and shabby and evidently has not been used in decades. The wallpaper is faded and the furnishings are decrepit and the springs coming out of the sofa. U. C. *there is a large fireplace with candelabra on either end of the mantelpiece. A large painting is above the fireplace. To the* R. *of it is a built-in bookcase. On a diagonal wall to the* R. *of this is a large arched opening with drapes at the side. Through the opening and to the* R. *is presumably the way to the front door. Immediately to the* L. *is a passage leading to a dining room and servant's pantry, etc. Leading off and* U. *is a staircase leading to the upstairs of the house. This entranceway should be on a one-step platform. Either side of the arch is a potted fern on a stand.* D. R. *is a door leading to a closet.* R. C. *is a desk perpendicular to the audience with a desk chair on the* R. *of it and a long, padded stool on the* C. *side of it. Directly* C. *is a large sofa with a standing ashtray to the* L. *of it and a long, narrow table above it. In front of the fireplace is a settee or bench which people can sit on. To the* L. *of the fireplace is a door which is not immediately apparent to the audience as it is covered with the same wallpaper and has paintings hanging on it. This leads*

9

directly to the butler's pantry and servants' quarters. Diagonally from this to the L. wall is a pair of French windows. Drapes are at either side but they never need be closed. Through the windows can be seen an extension of the house and a wall with sky beyond it. The D. L. wall has a rather ominous painting of a rather ominous character of the past century glaring down. In front of the painting is a long sofa perpendicular to the audience. There is room to move between the sofa and the wall. Cobwebs and dust hang from everywhere and the general effect is of a setting for a good murder story. In this first scene, since we are giving the impression it is a television studio, a pipe of spotlights or scoop lights is hanging down visible to the audience. They do not work. The tormentors L. and R. are removed and black legs are hung U. to shield the actors. A rather large floodlight is standing in the French windows, a work light on a stand D. L. A large TV cable runs from D. R. and out through the French windows. These effects are up to the discretion of the director but some of them should be used to give the effect needed and to show a difference when the rest of the play takes place on the actual island, in the real setting.

When the CURTAIN OPENS, *the stage is in DARK-NESS except for the WORK LIGHT D. L. which is on. It is a small-watt bulb and only gives off a little glow. Off U. L. there is the sound of someone falling over a chair.*

WHIT. (*Offstage.*) Dammit!

JESS. (*Off* U. R.) What happened?

WHIT. (*Off.*) I fell over something.

JESS. (*Off.*) Where are you?

WHIT. (*Off.*) How the hell do I know? It's like the Black Hole of Calcutta.

JESS. (*Off.*) Shall I send a St. Bernard?

WHIT. (*Off.*) I think I'm in a dressing room.

JESS. (*Off.*) There's a light over this way.

WHIT. (*Off.*) Well, follow the gleam.

JESS. (*Comes onstage humming the tune of "Follow the Gleam."* JESSICA OLIVE *is an extremely attractive and sophisticated woman in her middle thirties. To her, everything is a joke and a reason for a laugh. She is dressed in an attractive outfit with a turban-type hat which she later removes. She and her husband are the epitome of the rich, devil-may-care type of characters who used to be so prevalent in mystery stories and they play their characters to the hilt.* JESS *carries a large tote bag crammed with her necessities. She pauses in the archway.*) I've found it!

WHIT. What?

JESS. The gleam. I'm in a living room. It's straight out of "Dracula."

WHIT. (*Off.*) As long as there's electricity.

JESS. (*Sees a small chair and table to the* R. *of the fireplace. This furniture later gets moved to* D. R. *Crosses to it.*) And there's the most marvelous little Chippendale chair. It's exactly what we need in the hall. You know that space next to the table—

WHIT. (*Off.*) Jessica, it's rather disconcerting to find you more interested in Chippendale than your lost husband.

JESS. Stay where you are, darling. I'll flick on the lights.

WHIT. (*Off.*) That shows a level head.

JESS. (*Presses wall switch to the* R. *of the arch.*) Nothing happened.

WHIT. (*Off.*) Just keep talking. I'll find you.

JESS. What will I say?

WHIT. (*Off. Sound of him crashing into something again.*) Ow!

JESS. You're getting closer.

WHIT. (*Off.*) Keep talking. Count!

JESS. (*Crosses around the table and to* U. C., *looking over the room.*) Oh, dear. B-3. N-27. Under the O-64 . . .

WHIT. (*Appears in French windows carrying a lit cigarette lighter. He extinguishes it.* WHITNEY OLIVE *is a few years older than* JESS *and matches her in wit, sophistication, and graciousness. He is in the latest fashion and might have walked out of the pages of* Esquire.) Bingo!

JESS. (*Rushes to him at* U. L. *With put-on dramatic tones.*) Darling, you made it. After all this time, you found me. (*Holds him away from her.*) But you've aged. Oh, yes, you have. Silver threads and all that.

WHIT. Don't give me any of your outdated dialogue. Just an apology.

JESS. For what?

WHIT. For not following my advice and waiting until the others got here.

JESS. (*Crosses to table above sofa and lights candle.*) But it puts us a giant step ahead of them to see this room first. Now, you sit down over there and I'll find the lights.

WHIT. (*Sits on* L. *side of settee* C.) You said they didn't work.

JESS. (*Crosses to* D. R.) There must be a master switch somewhere. One of those enormous big levers. (*Exits* D. R. *below the flats.*)

WHIT. I wouldn't venture out there if I were you.

JESS. (*Off.*) I'm perfectly all right. The light board is always near the stage somewhere. (*SOUND of her falling over something.*) Ow!

WHIT. Good. We're even.

JESS. (*Off.*) I hope you've kept up my Blue Cross.

WHIT. Medicare takes you over in October.

JESS. (*Off.*) Ha! Ha!

WHIT. (*Looks around.*) My God, this is a dreary place.

JESS. (*Off.*) It's supposed to be. Sh, here we are.

WHIT. Find it?

JESS. (*Off.*) There are banks of little switches. **Ready?**

WHIT. (*Poses ready to be caught under a spotlight.*)
Go ahead.

JESS. (*As ONE SPOTLIGHT comes on far across
the stage from* WHIT.) How's that?

WHIT. Marvelous. If I were Laurence Olivier, I'd
never forgive you. Try another. (*Poses again.*)

JESS. This is number five. (*GREEN STRIP LIGHTS
come on.*)

WHIT. (*Getting exasperated.*) It's green. You've
made me look like Lon Chaney.

JESS. (*Offstage, excited.*) Oh, oh, oh, here it is. It's a
big lever. Here we go. (*LIGHTS full up. WORK
LIGHT goes off.*)

WHIT. (*Sees room completely.*) Jessica, this *is* a
dreadful room.

JESS. (*Comes from* D. R. *and up to* WHIT.) It's an
exact reproduction, so Mr. Summers said. (*As she enters.*) Oh, you're right. I wouldn't be caught dead here.
(*Blows out candle.*)

WHIT. Well, many people have been.

JESS. Oh, that's good, Whitney. Your sense of humor
is coming back. (*Sits beside him.*) Now, what will we
do? (*Puts tote bag on floor.*)

WHIT. Silly girl. Have a martini.

JESS. What a whoppingly brilliant idea. (*Pulls two
martini glasses out of tote bag.*)

WHIT. I thought you'd like it.

JESS. Here. Hold these.

WHIT. (*Takes them and looks around him.*) It does
sort of feel like we're in a living room, doesn't it?

JESS. (*As she pulls thermos of martinis out of tote
bag.*) Except the furniture's all wrong.

WHIT. It's depressing, but it's right for the set, I
gather.

JESS. (*As she pours the martinis into the glasses.*)
I mean it's placed wrong. Hasn't that ever annoyed you?
Everything is facing out there. (*Indicates front.*)

WHIT. It has to. That's where the audience is.

JESS. I know that. Oh, God, you are stupid. I mean,

if this were a real living room, the furniture would be in clusters.

WHIT. Conversational units, as you call them?

JESS. That's right. (*Thermos has gone back in bag and now she pulls out a small jar of pitted olives and a small fork.*) Olive?

WHIT. Naturally. (*She puts one in each glass, then puts things back in bag.*) If the furniture weren't facing the audience, then they wouldn't see the actors' faces.

JESS. Which would be a lot better in some cases.

WHIT. Naturalistic theatre, isn't it called?

JESS. Like that dreary little thing we saw off-Broadway.

WHIT. (*Laughing to himself.*) Parts of it were enjoyable.

JESS. You're a dirty old man.

WHIT. Granted.

JESS. (*Laughs, too.*) Whoever would invest in a nude version of "Hedda Gabler"?

WHIT. Other dirty old men. (*Toasts.*) What'll we drink to?

JESS. The project, of course.

WHIT. Good idea.

JESS. Here's to death, murder, violence, and mayhem.

WHIT. But with sophistication.

JESS. (*Nods.*) With sophistication. Cheers.

WHIT. Cheers. (*They drink.*) Now everything's right with the world.

JESS. (*Suddenly.*) Whitney!

WHIT. (*Jumps as he is startled.*) Don't do that.

JESS. Sorry, darling, but I suddenly thought of something chaotic. What happens if we don't like the others?

WHIT. One can't like everyone.

JESS. We signed the contract.

WHIT. It's good money.

JESS. You always have exactly the right phrase at the right time.

WHIT. Even if we despise the others, it will be good

to get back to work again. Me sitting at the typewriter, you pacing back and forth, trading ideas—

JESS. Bickering is what you mean.

WHIT. We don't really bicker, darling. Sometimes perhaps we have a slight disagreement.

JESS. Like the time you wanted to hurl a hatchet into that girl's back?

WHIT. Aren't you ever going to forget that?

JESS. It was such a bloody idea. Our readers would have closed the book then and there. From us, they expect pleasant murders. A simple poison, a quick shot in the dark, even a polite stab in the back if it's genteel like with a hatpin. But hatchets . . . really, Whit, you must have been drinking early that day.

WHIT. I was trying to change the pattern.

JESS. You don't change a pattern that pays off.

WHIT. Paid off.

JESS. Paid off. But people still read our books, don't they?

WHIT. In the dentist's office when they're through with the *National Geographic.*

JESS. We've got enough to be more than comfortable the rest of our lives and I don't regret one moment of it. (*Rises, puts her glass on the table above the sofa and crosses to the desk.*) But you're right. I'm getting excited about working again.

WHIT. It's time our style came back into vogue anyway.

JESS. We really brought murder to a new high, didn't we? (*Having glanced over the desk, she looks in the closet as she starts her thorough examination of the room.*) We were like an art gallery. All these new ones are like butcher shops.

WHIT. (*As JESS exits through arch.*) I wish someone else would get here. I feel rather stupid sipping a martini in an empty sound studio.

JESS. (*Off.*) It will soon be bustling with authors, don't worry. (*Comes in again. Touches the wall U. R.*) They certainly make these sets realistic, don't they?

WHIT. That's the point.

JESS. It's just canvas. I could swear it was a wall. And that ceiling. I suppose it's for acoustics.

WHIT. Probably. (*Calls.*) Helloooooo! See. No echo. (*From off* L. *we hear an answering "Helloooooo!" from* MILDRED.) My voice is changing!

JESS. (*Calls off.*) Over here. Follow the gleam.

MILDRED. (*Off.*) Be right with you. This is a gloomy vault, isn't it?

JESS. Wait until you get where we are.

WHIT. (*To* JESS.) It's a woman.

JESS. (*Takes her glass from above table.*) Must be Mildred Maxwell.

MILDRED. (*Enters through arch.* MILDRED Z. MAX-WELL *is a large woman, folksy in a way, but very de-termined and opinionated. She often has a sharp way of speaking although she is a friendly soul. She is in her late fifties or early sixties, wears a two-piece silk dress and a small hat. She carries a large bag with her which contains her handiwork.*) I made it. (*Shields her eyes from the lights.*) Oh, those lights are bright, aren't they?

JESS. Stand in the right color and it'll take ten years off you.

MILDRED. Nothing could do that short of a visit to Lourdes. (*Crosses to* JESS *with hand outstretched.*) How do you do. I am Mildred Z. Maxwell.

JESS. We've read everything you've ever written.

MILDRED. Why, thank you, dear. A few million more like you and I wouldn't have to be here now. (*Moves below and descends on* WHIT *who rises.*) You must be Mr. Summers.

WHIT. Wrong.

MILDRED. I hate to be wrong.

WHIT. Whitney Olive, and this is my wife, Jessica.

MILDRED. (*They shake hands.* JESS *moves above the desk and sits on the desk chair.*) Of course, I should have known. The martinis.

WHIT. Would you like one?

MILDRED. Never drink on a job, dear. Coagulates the mind. And let me say, *I* have read everything *you've* ever written.

WHIT. Now we're even,

MILDRED. But I had no idea you were so like your books.

JESS. In what way?

MILDRED. I mean, every one of your murders started out with a charming couple sipping a martini and then things happened. It was like a trademark.

JESS. We have to maintain the image.

WHIT. Besides, we happen to enjoy martinis.

MILDRED. (*Settles down on the sofa* L. *and takes her crocheting out of her bag and starts working on it.*) So do I, but, unfortunately, I never made a career out of it. Well, where are the others?

JESS. (*As* WHIT *sits on the sofa again.*) No one else has come yet.

MILDRED. Honestly, now, what do you think of this whole thing?

WHIT. Should be delightful fun if we don't all end up fighting.

MILDRED. Every bee to his own bonnet, as I always say.

JESS. I wondered what you always said.

MILDRED. (*Laughs.*) You *are* like your books. Marvelous. I wish I were. I try to be, but it never comes off somehow.

JESS. How do you mean?

MILDRED. My characters are so thoroughly organized and my plots so spectacularly logical, but in reality I have trouble balancing my checkbook. Never think it from my stories, would you?

WHIT. Certainly not. Those murders are brilliantly plotted. They're something like a geometry problem. Many's the time I've said to Jess that we could use more of your ingenuity.

MILDRED. And many's the time I've wished for your comic flair for the urbane.

JESS. (*Gets the thermos and refills* WHIT's *drink, then returns to the desk and refills her own.*) Whitney, this collaboration is going to be perfect. We're getting along like a house afire already.

MILDRED. Mutual respect, that's what all authors should have.

WHIT. Especially mystery authors who are dated.

MILDRED. Nonsense, we're not dated. Your stories are still as alive and thrilling as ever.

JESS. (*Puts thermos back in bag and sits on desk.*) But we only hinted at sex and we avoided violence whenever possible.

MILDRED. But mine are timeless. The unusual murder, the interfering detective and then call everyone into a room and give them the answer. That's the basis of all murder books.

WHIT. Not any more, I'm afraid. Take our characters, for instance—rich, sophisticated, always from the Four Hundred. What do you read about today? Pick up any murder mystery and every girl has bosoms like watermelons and rich, creamy thighs. I never wrote any girl like that.

JESS. He may have thought it, but he never wrote it.

MILDRED. We'll come back, my dears, just hang onto your typewriters. The pendulum is swinging. Even the sexy CIA agent with all his super weapons is out. I bet Brad Benedict hasn't sold a thousand copies of his latest.

(BRAD BENEDICT *enters through the arch from* U. L. *He is much younger than the others and, consequently, more mod in his dress but by no means "hippie." Actually,* BRAD *is a very shy and retiring person as we shall soon see. He has a quiet sense of humor that manifests itself in a small grin when he has been amusing, but usually he takes a back seat and admires the others. He comes in and moves to the* L. *end of the settee.*)

BRAD. I get my royalty statement next month but I think you may be right.

MILDRED. There I go again, putting my foot in it right up to the knee.

BRAD. It's O.K. It's true.

WHIT. (*Rises.*) How do you do. I'm—

BRAD. I know who you are, both of you. (*Shakes hands with both of them.*) You're the Olives. I always loved that name. It goes so well with martinis. And Miss Maxwell. A pleasure.

JESS. And you're Brad Benedict, the author who brought the transistor radio to the pencil and the camera to the cigarette lighter. (*Toasts him and sips.*)

BRAD. It was good while it lasted.

JESS. We were all complimenting each other on our murders. Would you care to join in?

BRAD. Am I expected to compliment my idols?

JESS. (*Delighted.*) Oh, I like that.

BRAD. Without you stalwarts of the murder mystery, I never would have had my short-lived career. I learned everything from you.

MILDRED. Now, that's a nice speech, dear. Sit down and join us.

WHIT. And have a martini. (*Sits.*)

BRAD. My pleasure. (*Sees no glass. Holds out his hand.*) Just a handful, please.

WHIT. Don't underestimate my wife. Jess, a glass.

(JESS *crosses below* BRAD *to her bag.*)

JESS. I always carry a spare for guests. (*Takes extra glass from bag, hands it to* BRAD *and pours.*)

BRAD. Jason Summers isn't here yet?

MILDRED. No, just the three of us. One thing we've already decided. (JESS *puts thermos back in bag.*) They may expect it but we're not going to fight. We'll collaborate peacefully and make a fortune.

BRAD. (*Sits on bench by desk.*) I'm all for that.

MILDRED. Just to clear the air, dear, I must say there's something about you I hate. It's not the modern

style you use. I concede that since you have a dynamic
flair. It's—well, it's your name.

BRAD. What's wrong with it? (*As* JESS *hands him
martini.*) Thanks.

MILDRED. (*As* JESS *sits on desk.*) The two B's. I
hate authors who have alliterative names.

BRAD. What about yours?

MILDRED. I predate you—unfortunately.

JESS. Ah, but you switched your name around, Mildred. I read it somewhere.

MILDRED. That damned *Reader's Digest.*

JESS. You were born Zelda Mildred and changed it to
make Mildred Z. Maxwell.

BRAD. Besides, Brad Benedict is my real name. Actually, it's Bradley Bruce Benedict. Are you ready for
that?

MILDRED. I .concede.

BRAD. Here's to you. (*Drinks.*) Good. You never get
them dry enough these days.

JESS. Whit has the secret.

BRAD. What?

WHIT. I pour the gin in the thermos and then close
it up and whisper the word "vermouth" in the next
room.

BRAD. (*Puts drink down and crosses to fireplace, cas-
ing the room.*) Say, this is quite a rotten old room,
isn't it?

MILDRED. (*Rises as she really looks at the room for
the first time.*) My agent told me it is an exact replica
of the one on the island. They're going to shoot the
script here.

WHIT. After we write it.

JESS. I hope we all work quickly. I hate to belabor
murder.

MILDRED. I once did one of my most successful books,
"The Golden Mummy Case," in six days.

BRAD. You must have worked non-stop.

MILDRED. No, I had hives and I couldn't sleep.
(*Crosses below bench.*)

JESS. There's no reason why we can't pop this thing out in a few days. I gather they want each of us to have a little of our own thing in the story so it will appeal to everyone.

WHIT. Some producer's smart idea.

MILDRED. My dears, we'll show them we're not through yet.

JESS. Show who? (*Rises and crosses to French windows.*) I think we're being stood up.

WHIT. Someone's bound to come soon. Just Summers and Duckton left.

(MILDRED *sits at desk and tries it out.*)

BRAD. (*At* U. R. *of settee.*) Say, whatever happened to Rodney Duckton?

JESS. (*Giggles.*) That sounds like a movie title, doesn't it? (*Acts it out grimly.*) Whatever happened to Rodney Duckton?

BRAD. No, really. I thought he was dead.

MILDRED. I'm sure he's not. I always read the obituary page first thing in the morning. It's a sign of age. (*Opens the desk drawers and looks through them.*)

WHIT. Now, he was one author who switched styles all right. After all those horror movie things, suddenly, in the thirties, he came up with Jack Club.

MILDRED. And made a mint, dear, with all those hard-hitting private eye stories. (*Rises.*) Probably retired to an island in the Caribbean.

JESS. I hope he has a better house than this one.

MILDRED. (*Walks toward closet.*) The real this one, you mean.

JESS. (*To* WHIT.) She is getting cryptic.

MILDRED. (*Turns at closet door.*) One thing I'll say for Duckton's books, though, he always had a good shock element in them.

WHIT. It kept the readers awake.

MILDRED. (*Opens closet door but keeps looking at the others.*) You never knew when you were going to come upon a—

RODNEY. Surprise! (MILDRED *has opened the door and* RODNEY DUCKTON *is standing there.* RODNEY *is the oldest of the authors but is extremely vital and constantly interested in everything that goes on. There develops a small rivalry between him and* MILDRED *and a small generation gap between him and* BRAD. RODNEY *is dressed impeccably and is always full of boundless enthusiasm and energy.* MILDRED *screams.*) I didn't mean to scare you. Really. I just wanted to make an entrance so I came round this way. (*Shakes* MILDRED'S *hand after closing closet door.*) Miss Maxwell, this is indeed a pleasure. I was just rereading your "The Case of the Blackeyed Turtle" last week and I do admire your structure.

JESS. (*Almost an aside to* WHIT.) I wish someone admired my structure.

WHIT. I do, dear.

JESS. Thank you, darling. (WHIT *has risen and patted her affectionately.*)

WHIT. (MILDRED *crosses above desk and back to sofa* L. *and her handiwork.* WHIT *crosses down to* RODNEY *and they meet below the desk.*) Mr. Duckton, after all these years, we meet. I am Whitney Olive and this is my wife, Jessica.

RODNEY. (*As they shake hands.*) I'm a tremendous fan of yours. Tremendous.

WHIT. Thank you. (*Moves toward* MILDRED.) Miss Maxwell you seem to know.

RODNEY. I kept that cover story in *Time* about her. Of course it was twenty years ago and she's changed somewhat. . . .

MILDRED. (*As she sits.*) And when did you leave Shangri-la?

RODNEY. I detect a note of bitterness which is not apparent in your writings. (BRAD *comes* D. C.) And this is Brad Benedict.

BRAD. How are you, sir?

RODNEY. (*They shake hands.*) A pity.

BRAD. What is?

RODNEY. You are me. Younger, of course. You took what I wrote in the thirties, added a few transistors, undressed a few women, and got astoundingly good royalties for a while.

BRAD. (*Crosses and sits on settee.*) That time was a few years ago.

RODNEY. (*Enthusiastically.*) So, we're all going to work together. I must say I'm looking forward to it, trading ideas, plots. When do we start?

WHIT. As soon as Mr. Summers gets here. (RODNEY *starts looking at the room, crosses below desk and* U. *of it.*) We've been waiting so long on this set, the tide is getting low in my martini thermos.

(JESS *sits on the couch.*)

RODNEY. Intriguing room, isn't it?

JESS. Dreary, I call it.

RODNEY. Ah, what I could have done with this in my horror days. (*He gestures throughout the following.*) A sliding panel here, a groping hand there, the beautiful girl seated at the desk. Footsteps coming down the corridor. She turns . . . screams . . . (*Drops the enthusiasm.*) But that doesn't scare anyone any more. Pity.

BRAD. Your Jack Club would have hit the monster over the head with the butt of his gun.

RODNEY. (*Crosses* L. *to settee.*) Ah, another era. Jack Club. Warner Brothers made a good thing out of him. But who and what are current now?

WHIT. Nothing. That's why we're all here.

RODNEY. What do we do now?

JESS. If anyone else says that, I shall call a cab and go home.

(JASON SUMMERS *enters through the arch. He is a man in his thirties, efficient looking right down to his horn-rimmed glasses which he occasionally takes off to emphasize a point. He is dressed in a neat, Madison Avenue suit.* JASON *is enthusiastic about the project before him but terrified that it will go wrong and he will lose his job; hence there is an extreme nervous quality about him plus an always eager-to-please-everyone attitude. He carries a speaker's podium and a pile of file cards.*)

JASON. Good evening, everyone. I am Jason Summers, the man who contacted your respected agents.

ALL. (*As they rise.*) How do you do. We've been waiting for you. (*Etc., etc.*)

JASON. (*Places the podium* D. R. *corner of the stage, then comes up to the authors and shakes hands with them quickly, moving from* R. *to* L. *At one point, he trips slightly over the television cable.*) I purposely came a little late to let you all get acquainted. Clever idea, wasn't it? Actually, the vice-president in charge of new shows suggested it. I can't take all the credit, can I? (*By now, he is by* JESS.)

JESS. Why not?

JASON. They'd find out. Jealousy, you know. (*Moves back to podium.*) Now, shall we get started? (*Puts the file cards on the podium and addresses the audience.*) Good evening, ladies and gentlemen. Welcome to WMT Studios.

JESS. (*As the authors look at each other quizzically.*) Who's he talking to?

WHIT. I don't know.

JASON. It is our pleasure to invite you to join us in a short experimental evening in crime.

BRAD. (*As the authors become more perplexed.*) He's not speaking to us.

JASON. (*Continuing out front, trying to ignore the interruptions.*) Down through the ages, murder and mayhem have fascinated each and every one of us.

MILDRED. Maybe he's psychotic.

JASON. So tonight we have brought together the outstanding mystery writers of their time.

RODNEY. (*Crosses below desk, trying to interrupt him.*) Mr. Summers—

JASON. It is our idea to—

RODNEY. Mr. Summers—

JASON. (*To audience.*) Excuse me. (*To* RODNEY.) Yes, Mr. Duckton.

RODNEY. We're all wondering one thing.

JASON. What?

RODNEY. Who the hell are you talking to?

JASON. To the audience.

RODNEY. What audience?

JASON. Out there. (*Indicates the audience.*)

RODNEY. (*Shields his eyes from the lights as he looks out front. He sees them.*) Good God, you're right! There are people out there.

(*The authors all look out front and are shocked to see people there.* BRAD *comes* D. *and immediately walks back* U. *again as he is terrified of so many people.* WHIT *comes down to footlights and remains there. The authors all react differently to the audience,* JESS *and* WHIT *enjoying them the most, although none of the authors approves of the audience being there.*)

BRAD. Lots of them!

WHIT. My God!

JESS. (*Pulls compact from her bag.*) And I look a fright.

MILDRED. (*Crosses to* JASON.) Mr. Summers, what is the meaning of this?

WHIT. Is this a joke?

JASON. Didn't your agents tell you there would be an audience?

WHIT. Certainly not, or I would have worn black tie.

JASON. Perhaps it's an oversight on my part. However, there's no harm done, is there? This is just an experiment. More of a game really. (*He keeps smiling out at the audience as the others play between themselves and the audience.*)

MILDRED. (*Offended.*) Murder is hardly a game. We all have made a career out of it.

JASON. Please sit down and let me explain.

BRAD. (*Sits on the settee* C.) I'm no good in front of audiences. People make me nervous.

(WHIT *sits on the bench.* JESS *sits on the settee with* BRAD. RODNEY *helps* MILDRED *to the sofa* L. *and sits* U. *of her.*)

JESS. I think we should all go home.

WHIT. No, I'm fascinated. Let's hear him out.

RODNEY. (*Looks at audience as they all do.*) They look like nice people, but there are so many of them.

JASON. (*Again to audience.*) Sorry about this delay, but authors are temperamental, too, the same as actors and everyone else connected with the creative arts. As I was saying, look at these five people, ladies and gentlemen. (*He gestures and turns to them. They are all glaring at him.*) What do you see? Genius! That's what you see. Five brains which have been dedicated to murder.

JESS. Don't tempt us.

JASON. (*Ignores this.*) WMT Studios has brought together, at great expense, these five minds to collaborate and become one, to bring you the great mystery series of all time, what we hope will be television's finest hour. Now, let me introduce them to you—the faces behind the book jackets, as it were. (*He has a forced laugh.*)

RODNEY. (*To* MILDRED *as* JASON *shuffles his file notes.*) Does he write his own material?

JASON. Jessica and Whitney Olive, authors of over thirty best sellers, former joint presidents of the Crime Writers' League, and the darlings of International Society. (JESS *and* WHIT *rise and face front. They bow.*) You may applaud, if you wish. (*Applauds and hopefully the audience picks it up.*)

WHIT. (*Toasts with martini.*) Thank you.

JESS. (*With a glare at* JASON.) I can't tell you how I feel being here. (*Gives a rather hollow smile to the audience.*)

JASON. Thank you. (WHIT *and* JESS *sit again.*) Mildred Z. Maxwell, specialist in the surprise ending, the woman who (MILDRED *rises with a look of despair at* RODNEY.) has kept us up at night waiting for the final page of her latest mystery. (*She bows.*)

MILDRED. (*Pointedly at* JASON.) I'm constantly thinking of a new way to kill people. (*Sits.*)

JASON. Brad Benedict, the man who modernized the spy. His heroes are hard-hitting and perform with no holds barred, whether it's with the enemy or with a beautiful woman.

BRAD. (*After* JESS *prods him, he rises quickly and shyly.*) Thank you. (*Reseats himself quickly.*)

JASON. And finally, Rodney Duckton, the gentleman who terrified us when we were young with such monsters as the Creeping Fiend, the Crawling Hand, and the Ghoulish Girl, and who later went on to create the master private eye of the thirties, the one and only two-fisted and two-gunned Jack Club.

RODNEY. (*Rises and bows.*) It was nothing really, just an extension of myself. You see —

WHIT. (*Realizing* RODNEY *is prepared for a long speech.*) Oh, do sit down. (*After a glare at* WHIT, RODNEY *sits again.*)

JASON. It is my idea, or rather the idea of the WMT Studios—

JESS. Watch that or you'll get fired.

JASON. —to combine these talents, to put a little Maxwell here, a splash of Benedict there, a dose of Duckton, a few dashes of Olives, and come up with a tossed salad of murder.

WHIT. Block that metaphor.

JASON. This stage setting which you see before you is an exact reproduction of the living room of Vulture's Vault.

MILDRED. Does everything have to be alliterative?

JASON. (*Showing he is upset at the authors, although he continues to ignore them.*) From the time when buccaneers sailed the Spanish Main, there has been a house on a small island off Jamaica which has been shrouded with mystery. That house is called Vulture's Vault. That famous pirate, Redbeard, built it with slave labor, stored his riches there, and died in the very room we have copied for you. During the twenties, Vulture's Vault was used as a storage depot for liquor being run illegally into the United States. (*One of his cards is out of order, which causes him a momentary embarrassed pause while he shuffles cards.*) Sold in 1931 to Morgan Fitzby, it was the island where the multimillionaire recluse met his unfortunate end—a knife protruding from his back.

MILDRED. This dialogue is terrible.

JESS. (*With a look to the audience.*) Appalling.

JASON. (*Crosses L. to MILDRED.*) Miss Maxwell, I am not a successful author like you. Your turn will come.

RODNEY. If he doesn't shut up soon, the audience will leave. (*Smiles at them.*)

JESS. (*To the audience.*) Hang on, it can't get much worse.

WHIT. (*To audience.*) If there are any reviewers out there, that's what is known as a quotable line.

JASON. (*Tries to laugh it off. Crosses between settee and desk.*) As you can see, we're all very informal at this gathering. (*Moves back D. R.*) Tonight our authors will get acquainted with each other and their working methods. It will just be a little fun.

BRAD. I hate games.

RODNEY. I rather fancy myself at cribbage, and—

JASON. Mr. Duckton—

RODNEY. Sorry.

JASON. Immediately following this show, our five authors will be flown to the Caribbean where tomorrow they will travel by small boat to Vulture's Vault. There, ladies and gentlemen, they will create—create stories of suspense, intrigue, and murder. A series rivaled by none in the history of television. (*Pauses as he waits. Dis-*

appointed.) Oh, dear, I rather expected a little applause there.

WHIT. And another copywriter's head will fall.

JESS. Do be quiet, darling, this might be fun.

JASON. The series will be shot here on this very set with the leading actors of a bygone era. WMT is going to bring back stars who, along with these authors, you have almost forgotten.

(*This offends the authors immeasurably and they all rise. The following six speeches are said in unison.*)

JASON. Please, authors, please.

WHIT. That does it!

BRAD. Passe at thirty-two.

JESS. Grab the thermos, Whit, we're leaving.

MILDRED. I could commit murder now!

RODNEY. I loathe honesty in the young.

JASON. Let me remind you of the ironclad contracts our lawyers have drawn up. (*This quiets the authors.*) And also the salaries you are being paid. *And* the fact that your combined sales in the past two years haven't equaled one month of the country's best seller, "Sex For Profit."

WHIT. (*As they reseat themselves.*) Is the thermos empty?

MILDRED. I could drink hemlock.

RODNEY. Jack Club would blast his way out of here.

BRAD. (*To* RODNEY.) I should have planted a honing device on him last week. (*Stands by settee.* WHIT *fills glasses as* JESS *holds them, then* WHIT *sits on settee.*)

JASON. Now for our get acquainted game. The envelope, please. (*A hand comes out of the wings from* D. R. *holding a large, white envelope.*)

JESS. This is too much.

RODNEY. Price-Waterhouse is everywhere.

JASON. Thank you. Inside here are twelve slips of paper. Each slip has one word on it. That word is the motive. There are such things as lust, greed, money, etc. (*Moves toward sofa* L.) I shàll have you, Miss Maxwell, pick one paper.

MILDRED. (*To* RODNEY *as she rises.*) I like Password better.

JASON. Then you can toss the motive around until you come up with a plot. We shall watch your minds mesh together on your first collaboration. (*To audience.*) Isn't this exciting?

JESS. Are *we* allowed to answer?

JASON. No! Then, with this and the publicity we shall get when you all arrive at Vulture's Vault, the series will be pre-sold.

RODNEY. When do we start work?

JASON. The day after you arrive. After an early morning press conference you will be left completely alone to create.

JESS. (*Rises and moves down to* JASON'S L.) Wait a minute. Who creates in the kitchen? The only thing I do properly is Quiche Lorraine.

MILDRED. What cheese do you use? Swiss or Gruyère?

JESS. Gruyère, of course. I find it doesn't—

JASON. You will have the proper retinue of servants. Your only responsibility is to bring back thirteen plots in three weeks. (JESS *sits on the settee.*) All right, Miss Maxwell, draw a motive.

MILDRED. This is deadlier than the draft lottery. (*Draws one paper.*)

JASON. Read it, please.

MILDRED. (*With a deadly gleam.*) Murder Jason Summers.

JESS. Goody.

JASON. I beg your pardon.

MILDRED. Just trying for a little humor.

BRAD. (*Crosses behind the sofa* L.) Someone's got to entertain those people.

MILDRED. It says, "Jealousy."

WHIT. That's as original as sin.

JASON. (*Crosses* R. *of the settee and up to the fender in front of the fireplace and sits at end of speech.*) Perfect. Now, I'll just disappear over here in the corner and you can start plotting.

RODNEY. (*There is a long pause as* MILDRED *moves* U. L. *and the others try to think, with occasional glances at the audience.*) I can't just sit here and think up a plot. I always do my best work in the early morning.

BRAD. I have to slouch in a chair for weeks before I come up with something workable. (*Sits on sofa beside* RODNEY.)

WHIT. (*To audience.*) If you want to go out and have a smoke or something, we'll ring a bell when we have a good jealousy plot.

JESS. I'm jealous of anyone who isn't here.

MILDRED. (*To corner of settee.*) I have an old plot that's been kicking around for some time. I'll give it to you and then we can toss it around.

WHIT. There's that salad again.

MILDRED. (*As* JASON *takes her by the shoulders and guides her to podium. Then he sits on fender again.*) Well . . . here goes. (*To audience.*) I hope none of you paid to get in here.

WHIT. The press always gets passes.

MILDRED. Then they're getting their money's worth. Now, all I've worked out on this plot is the middle and the end. (*Leans over podium directly to audience.*) By the way, I hope you'll all read my books. They're available in paperback, you know, unless, of course, you like hardcover.

JASON. (*The authors are all exchanging disapproving glances and he half-rises.*) Miss Maxwell, please. No commercials.

MILDRED. All right, dear. Well, here's my plot. We have the usual husband who married a woman for her money. She is rich, prominent, and a bitch— (*To* JASON.) Oh, am I allowed to say words like that?

JASON. Censorship is at a new low; however, on the show we would simply call her a bad woman.

MILDRED. All right, then, the wife is a "bad woman."
She is tired of the husband and is about to divorce him.
He'll be left with nothing so, naturally, this being a
murder story, he decides to kill her. (*Ad-libs from the
authors showing disapproval of the usual plot.*) I realize all this is very usual so far, but Mildred Z. Maxwell always has surprises up her typewriter. This husband . . . Oh, dear, I can't tell stories well. I wish you
could see the characters as I do.

JASON. (*Rises and comes to corner of desk.*) Oh, but
they can, Miss Maxwell. Just use your imagination. Describe them and we shall see them. (*Sits again.*)

(*LIGHTS fade to a spot on* MILDRED *at the podium.*)

MILDRED. I'll try. The husband plots out the murder
most ingeniously. He has gotten hold of a third cousin
or an old ne'er-do-well classmate or someone like that
and is paying him to be an accomplice. (GEORGE *enters
through arch and stands above desk.*) This middle scene
I have worked out is between the two men. The husband, we'll call him George, should be good-looking in a
way, dressed in a nice suit, and— (*AREA LIGHT
above desk comes up on* GEORGE. *Since this is typical
of one of* MILDRED'S *earlier stories, the characters are
dressed in the period of the thirties.* GEORGE *is in a
bright pin-stripe suit, an overcoat slung over his shoulder. He wears a wide-brimmed slouch hat, sunglasses,
and smokes with a cigarette holder. He speaks in a very
smooth, oily voice.*) That's it. That's exactly what he
should look like. Isn't imagination wonderful? (*Crosses
up to him and examines him. He is frozen. The authors
are intensely interested.*)

WHIT. That's an appallingly bad suit. The cut—
JESS. Sh, this is her story.
WHIT. Sorry.
MILDRED. He *is* nice-looking. Oh, I forgot. He has
broken his arm. (*Indicates his left arm which is in a
cast and sling. To audience.*) That's a most important

plot point. (*Returns to the podium as the* MAN *saunters in through the French windows. By the time he reaches the area lighting, we realize we can see very little of him as he, too, wears an overcoat, dark glasses, smokes, and has his coat collar turned up. When he speaks, it is obvious he is of a much lower class than* GEORGE.) Now for the ne'er-do-well. He is, of course, ne'er-do-well looking. (*Turns and sees him.*) That's right. Perfect. George is just finishing plotting his intriguing murder. He says . . .

(*MUSIC suddenly blares forth. Perhaps it is the opening of Beethoven's Fifth. The authors look around for the source of the music.* GEORGE *turns and moves in to desk.*)

GEORGE. . . . and that's all you have to do. (*Pulls plane ticket from his sling.* MAN *takes it.*) Here's your plane ticket to Chicago made out in my name.

MAN. (*At* L. *of desk.*) You're sure nothin' can go wrong?

GEORGE. I've worked out even the smallest detail.

MILDRED. (*To audience.*) I haven't yet, of course, but I shall. (MAN *sits on bench by desk.*)

GEORGE. You will wear a cast and a sling. That will make you immediately identifiable. Get on the eleven o'clock plane, slouch down in your seat and pretend to sleep all the way. No one will pay attention to what you look like, just that you have the broken arm. Tomorrow, there will be eighty-some odd passengers who will swear I was on Flight 752 at the time of the murder.

MAN. (*As he puts the ticket in his coat pocket.*) Let us hope so.

GEORGE. It's fool-proof. At eleven-thirty, while you are somewhere between New York and Chicago, I shall get rid of Martha. And there's nothing the authorities can prove. (*Flicks ash in tray on desk.*) I am the one with the best motive, but I was apparently thirty thousand feet above the ground at the time it happened. A perfect alibi. (MILDRED *turns and gives a significant nod to the audience.*) I shall take the twelve-thirty flight to Chicago under an assumed name and be there when Martha's body is discovered. I shall be properly shocked, attend the funeral as a dutiful husband should, and inherit the estate oh, so reluctantly. (*Sits in desk chair.*) And there's not a thing Roger will be able to prove.

MAN. Roger is the new man?

GEORGE. Oh, yes, Martha always has a new man ready, willing, and younger.

MAN. You're sure they can't connect me with you in any way?

GEORGE. How could they? As far as anyone knows, we haven't seen each other in fifteen years.

MAN. (*Rises.*) There's only one thing you've overlooked.

GEORGE. Which is?

MAN. The money. (*His hands on the desk, he leans in to* GEORGE.)

GEORGE. (*Rises, pulls large, stuffed envelope from his pocket and hands it to the* MAN.) It's all here.

MAN. I'll be thinking of you at eleven-thirty tonight. (*Starts to slowly stroll out through the French windows.*)

GEORGE. And I'll be thinking of the future. (*LIGHTS BLACKOUT on* GEORGE *and he disappears out the arch. MUSIC goes OFF.*)

MILDRED. As I said, I've also worked out the climax at eleven-thirty that night. Martha, the wife, is at home. I suppose she'd best be dressed in a negligee. They always seem to be. And she'd better be lovely, but a trifle hard-looking. (*LIGHT area above desk comes on and there is* MARTHA *exactly as* MILDRED *has described her. She is wearing a stunning negligee, her hair is done in a severe style and she is well bejeweled. She is facing* U. *and holds the receiver of the desk phone in her hand.*) Oh, very good. Yes, that's Martha. Perhaps she is talking with this Roger . . .

MARTHA. (*Turns as she talks.*) Yes, Roger, darling . . .

MILDRED. Wait a minute. (MARTHA *freezes right in the middle of a gesture.*) We need more atmosphere. A radio. Soft music in counterpoint to the scene we know is coming. Can I have a radio, please?

JASON. Anything you wish. (*Rises and calls.*) Radio! (*A GRIP comes in from the arch carrying a small radio which he places on the desk.*)

MILDRED. What service. Thank you.

GRIP. You're welcome. (*Starts off.*)

MILDRED. It should be playing music.

GRIP. (*As he exits through arch, he calls off.*) Hey, Charlie. Music!

(*MUSIC comes on playing something sensuous, perhaps "Bolero."*)

MILDRED. Martha is on the phone.

MARTHA. (*Unfreezes.*) He's gone. A quick divorce and then we'll be together. . . . No, he leaves on the eleven o'clock flight from Newark Airport. . . . (*Laughs.*) The poor thing won't be able to carry all his luggage with that broken arm. He'll have to tip a skycap. That will really hurt him. . . . What? Mexico, I think. Divorces overnight. (*Lights a cigarette from a pack on the desk.*) Of course you can, darling. I wouldn't dream of going alone. . . . First thing in the morning, Roger. Why not lunch at one? . . . Pick me up here. Till then. . . . Yes, I am, too. (*Blows a kiss into the phone, hangs up. Exhales a long puff. She hears footsteps coming down the stairs in the arch.*) Hello— is someone there? Who is it?

GEORGE. (*Enters through arch in area lighting.*) Hello, Martha.

MARTHA. (*Crosses around desk and sits on bench.*) What are you doing here? Did you get drunk and miss the plane?

GEORGE. Not at all. I have never been more sober in my life.

MARTHA. You know, I don't think I have ever seen you sober.

GEORGE. (*Moves to above* MARTHA. *All of these trite lines are said by the characters with tremendous intensity as they are "taking off" the usual situations.*) Take a good look.

MARTHA. (*Turns and looks at him.*) You are sober. Is it because you have to buy your own Scotch now? You can get out. I've had my last look at you.

GEORGE. How right you are.

MARTHA. (*Turns to him.*) And just what does that mean?

GEORGE. I'm going to kill you. (*Pulls out revolver from his sling.*)

MARTHA. (*Laughs, rises and moves* D. R. *of desk.*) Don't be ridiculous.

GEORGE. I'm serious, Martha. Do you think I'm going to give up the job of being your husband without any retirement plan? (*Moves* D.)

MARTHA. You didn't retire. You were fired. Now get out of here. You can't scare me. Go on. Get on another plane. (*Puts cigarette out.*)

GEORGE. But I'm on one already. You see, Martha, there is someone flying over the country right now dressed like me with a broken arm. I have any number of witnesses who will swear I am not here but there. (*Moves below the desk. Turns RADIO volume up higher.*) It's all beautifully thought out.

MARTHA. (*To* U. R. *corner of desk.*) You're bluffing. Get out of here now or I'll call the police. (*Picks up phone.*)

GEORGE. You won't have time. (*Is at* D. R. *corner of desk.*)

MARTHA. I know you too well. You might think up something like this, but you'd never have the guts to pull it off. (*Dials.*)

GEORGE. You're wrong, Martha. (*Fires and the gun goes off.* MARTHA *falls to the floor. He kneels beside her for a moment, then replaces the receiver in the cradle.*)

(*The MUSIC stops abruptly and a* RADIO ANNOUNC-
ER'S VOICE *is heard.*)

ANNOUNCER. We interrupt this program for a news
bulletin. Amalgamated Airlines Flight 752 from Newark to Chicago has crashed outside of Cleveland, Ohio.
There are no survivors.

(GEORGE *turns front, shocked. LIGHTS BLACKOUT
except for the podium light on* MILDRED. GEORGE
and MARTHA *leave through the arch.*)

MILDRED. Surprise ending! I'm famous for them.
Shock it to them with the last line. Do I get applause
for that? (*Pauses to see if audience applauds.*) I should
hope so. (*LIGHTS DIM up on main room.*) Of course
there are lots of details to figure out, but we have our
jealousy—the husband jealous of Roger, and the money
which would rightfully be George's. What do you think?
(*Moves in c. a few steps.*)

RODNEY. (*The authors are all obviously far from
happy.*) I think it's nice, but—

MILDRED. (*Defensively.*) What?

RODNEY. There's no one you really care about.

MILDRED. I never really cared about anyone in your
books.

RODNEY. Now, now, now, let's not get testy. I always
had a sympathetic ingenue in there somewhere.

JESS. Perhaps if they were nicer people. Suppose we
met them at a cocktail party, for instance, and there's
some amusing chit-chat.

WHIT. That's not the way Mildred writes, Jess.

JESS. Well, we're collaborating, aren't we?

BRAD. (*Rises and faces* RODNEY.) Why don't we up-
date it? If George were with the CIA and he knew that
Roger was a spy for some foreign power, then he could
plant a honing device under Roger's lapel and overhear
them making love. Be rather a sexy scene. (*To the
audience.*) Audiences love that sort of thing.

MILDRED. Sex should be kept in the bedroom and not flaunted on television screens in the living room.

RODNEY. (*Rises and crosses to* MILDRED.) Why not make it a really good horror story? They used to play well and maybe it's time for a comeback. (*Crosses below* MILDRED *to podium.* BRAD *sits on sofa* L.) If this were one of those silent movies I used to write— Miss Maxwell, I'll show you.

MILDRED. Monsters are out, Mr. Duckton, they really are. (*Sits on sofa* L.)

RODNEY. But my climactic scenes are classics. They don't make them like that any more. Remember Frankenstein, Dracula? Well, I was way ahead of those boys. (*The LIGHTS in the room dim to the podium light and the same DESK AREA LIGHT.*) Lon Chaney and the silents. That's when we really had terror. We always had a mad scientist and he was always jealous because the ingenue loved another. Now, the ingenue is this beautiful girl. (*The* GIRL *enters down the stairs and to the* L. *of the desk, where she poses appropriately. She is dressed in an outfit of the late twenties, her hair is frizzy like a typical "It Girl," her eyes are large, and she has a Cupid's bow mouth. She is the pure ingenue of the period.*) Ah, magnificent! The mad scientist pleads once more for her hand in marriage. If refused, he will call in the monster he has created—to kill her. You'll note the ingenue doesn't see the monster until the last possible moment. Suspense! Now, for the scientist— (*He crosses to the arch as if to call one in, then turns.*) In all modesty, I must say that I don't think I could conjure up as good a mad scientist as I myself would make.

JESS. Whit and I do that. We're always acting things out.

WHIT. I fancy myself the John Gielgud type.

JESS. Really. I never noticed.

RODNEY. Please! (*To audience.*) Of course you must remember that I still think of these plots in terms of silent films and those wonderful title cards. Dialogue was so unimportant. Music provided the atmosphere. (*Calls.*) Music! (*MUSIC comes on. It is a deep, dramatic organ selection such as mad scientists always played.*) Ready. Action. (*RODNEY slips out the arch and to the* L. *The LIGHTS start FLICKERING, giving the effect of a silent movie. In this "take-off," the actors move in exaggerated movements with exaggerated gestures, giving the effect of a silent picture. The* GIRL *paces below the desk and to* C., *her hands wringing together in despair.* RODNEY *reenters in the usual long white coat of the scientist. He sees her, makes a quick move to her, crossing below the desk from the* R. *She turns and sees him. He gets on his knees, his hands in front of him. They freeze as the* GRIP *enters through the arch, comes between them and holds a placard which says, in old-fashioned printing, "WILL YOU BE MINE?" He holds it for a moment and goes off.* GIRL *crosses below* RODNEY *to* D. R. *He follows on his knees. He pulls on her skirts. She resists.* GRIP *enters with placard, which he holds between them. It says, "NO!"* GRIP *exits.* GIRL *rushes away to* D. C. RODNEY *crosses to arch after giving a cackling laugh face. He turns in arch.* GRIP *enters with placard saying, "THEN THIS SHALL BE YOUR FATE!"* GRIP *exits.* RODNEY *gestures off* R. *The* MONSTER *enters. He can be either made up horribly or else wearing one of those rubber Frankenstein masks and rubber hands. He is very tall and his height is added to because he is wearing built-up shoes or boots.* RODNEY *gestures to the* GIRL. *The* MONSTER *starts toward her,* RODNEY *cackles, and exits* L. *The* GIRL *appears to be picking flowers happily. She sits on the desk bench. The* MONSTER *comes toward her, his arms outstretched. Just as he is about to grab her, she rises and moves* D. R. *He follows, almost reaches her, and she moves below him to* D. C. *He moves to her. She turns, sees him, the* GRIP *enters and holds up a sign between them which reads, "SCREAM!" The* GIRL *gives a screaming look, spins in a complete circle, and faints. The* MONSTER *catches her and carries her through*

the arch and off R. *MUSIC OFF and BLACKOUT.*
RODNEY *comes through the arch and to the podium. He
has removed the white coat. When the LIGHTS come
UP on the room, he is looking wistfully front. The authors are all in a state of laughter.*) They don't make
them that way any more.

JESS. (*Laughing.*) They certainly don't.

RODNEY. (*To* JESS.) Are you laughing or choking?

JESS. It's funny.

WHIT. Jess, show some respect.

BRAD. What you've just shown us is what we call
"camp."

RODNEY. Camp?

WHIT. Mr. Duckton, you see what you did, don't
you?

RODNEY. (*Offended.*) Evidently not.

WHIT. (*Rises and moves* D. *to* C.) You've really done
a parody on your own work. To have the audience be
frightened of that, you'd have to have the audience of
the era. (*To audience.*) You're not that old, are you?

RODNEY. (*Moves in toward* WHIT.) They have
changed, haven't they?

WHIT. That's the trouble. You changed, too, when
you gave up horror and introduced Jack Club. That
started the hard-hitting era of detectives, but that would
be a parody now, too.

RODNEY. You really think so?

WHIT. Of course. I'll show you.

RODNEY. I don't think I want you to.

WHIT. But I'd enjoy it. (*To audience.*) I've been
quivering on the sidelines waiting to get into the act.
(*Moves* RODNEY *to below settee as he heads for arch.*)
You go over there and Jess and I will show you what
your Jack Club would be like now.

JESS. Goody. (*Rises and sits* RODNEY *on the settee.*)
I'm a marvelous actress.

RODNEY. Do you think this will accomplish anything?

MILDRED. Give them a chance.

JESS. (*Crosses to* WHIT.) Can we do it alone, Whit?

WHIT. We may have to call on a figment or two like the others. Now, I'll be Jack Club and you play the usual girl. All right? (JESS *exits through arch and off* R. WHIT *takes off his jacket and puts it on back of the desk chair, rolls up his sleeves.*)

JASON. (*Comes D. a few steps.*) Ladies and gentlemen, I feel I must apologize.

MILDRED. What for?

JASON. (*Crosses L. to* MILDRED.) This isn't exactly what we planned on. This is more of a happening than a mystery seminar. (*To others.*) You haven't collaborated yet.

BRAD. (*Takes* JASON *by the shoulders and pushes him back above the settee to his original place and seats him.*) Sit down! You got us here, so now let us do our thing. (*Sits beside* RODNEY.)

JASON. This isn't what I had in mind at all.

WHIT. (*At the podium.*) Jack Club stories always started with narration setting the hard-hitting scene, as it were. (*Podium LIGHT comes UP on him as LIGHTS in the room dim and the desk area LIGHT comes UP. MUSIC comes in. It is a slow, jazzy number with a blues trumpet playing.* WHIT *speaks in low monotone typical of the heroes of the day.*) It was a cold morning and the city was cold steel, like every heart in it. It had been a tough night. Violence was my friend. My name is Jack Club. (*Sits at desk and takes liquor bottle from desk drawer.*) I started out the day with my usual daycap. (*Takes swig from bottle and replaces it in desk drawer.*) Then suddenly I felt this tight knot in my gut. That was a sign this wasn't going to be an ordinary day. I waited. Then she came in. (*Pauses. MUSIC OUT.*) She came in!

JESS. (*Off.*) Oh, sorry, darling. Once again.

WHIT. Then she came in. (*MUSIC IN for* JESS. *It is a sensuous number and she keeps rhythm to it. She has her hair down, falling over her face. A small beret is on her head and she wears a matching trench coat. She leans against the U. wall of the arch in a provoca-*

tive pose.) She was bad. All bad. Her lips formed a wicked smile. (*They do.*) She was curvy and built like some Venus de Milo. (JESS' *arms climb up the arch to over her head.*) But she had arms. Arms that had held men—many men. I got up. (*He does and moves* L. *of desk.*) She came towards me like a bulldozer clearing a garbage dump. (*She comes* D. *to him.*) Her eyes searched me like a Geiger counter. (*Her eyes search him from head to toe.*) Then she spoke.

JESS. (*MUSIC OUT.*) I'm in trouble. Big trouble.

WHIT. My name is trouble.

JESS. (*Arms around his neck.*) Kiss me. Kiss me hard. (*He throws her in front of him and they go into a deep embrace. He pulls her up immediately to the same position.*)

WHIT. You're bad. All bad.

JESS. My husband is dead.

WHIT. I'm falling for you, baby. I'm falling fast. (*Another deep embrace exactly the same.*)

JESS. They think I shot him.

WHIT. Did you?

JESS. (*Crosses below him to* D. C.) What do you think?

WHIT. I think you're bad. All bad. (*Crosses to her.*)

JESS. It was his stepdaughter, Stephanie. (*Her arms around his neck.*) She's just my age. She shot him because he threatened to leave his money to me. Kiss me quick. (*They kiss.*)

WHIT. I've got it bad, baby.

JESS. You're tough, Jack Club. All tough. (*Her hands on his cheek.*)

WHIT. Where is this broad, Stephanie?

(*The closet door opens and* STEPHANIE *quickly closes it behind her and leans against it. She is young and innocent but there is a certain worldliness about her. She is very attractive.*)

STEPHANIE. Stephanie Mildaur, that's me.

JESS. She's rotten. All rotten.

WHIT. But innocent. So innocent.

STEPHANIE. (*Crosses to* WHIT.) That woman killed my father.

JESS. (WHIT *turns to* STEPHANIE *and* JESS *puts her arms on his back and points to* STEPHANIE.) It was you. All you.

STEPHANIE. (*To* WHIT.) Believe me. Please believe me.

WHIT. (*Pulls* STEPHANIE *to him.*) I do, baby.

JESS. But what of us? Our love? Our desires?

WHIT. (*Throws* JESS *away toward* C.) It's over, baby. All over.

JESS. (*Grabs his arm.*) What was my mistake?

WHIT. Putting your hand on my cheek. It's there. All there.

JESS. What is?

WHIT. Powder burns. (*Grabs her hand.*) From the gun you used to shoot your husband.

JESS. (*Backs away from him and pulls small revolver from her pocket.*) I'm sorry it had to end like this.

STEPHANIE. (*Throws herself between* JESS *and* WHIT.) Don't. Don't shoot him.

JESS. (*Saying it.*) Bang!

STEPHANIE. (*Falls back in* WHIT'S *arms. She is held up by his* R. *arm.*) Ahh!

WHIT. (*Looks at her.*) She's dead. All dead.

JESS. (*Crosses in to him.*) Forget about her, Jack Club. It can be you and me now.

WHIT. It's no good, baby. The memory of Stephanie Mildaur would always haunt us. (*Reaches for the gun.*) Give me that.

JESS. (*As they struggle for it.*) No!

WHIT. Yes! (*They struggle and he says:*) Bang!

JESS. (*Freezes as she is hit.*) I underestimated you, Jack Club. You're hard. All hard. (*She falls into his right arm. He now has one girl on each arm.*)

WHIT. Poor Stephanie. She was good. All good.

JESS AND STEPHANIE. (*They rise up simultaneously,*

their faces close to his cheek.) Jack . . . I love you
. . . let me go with a kiss.

WHIT. (*Kisses* STEPHANIE *and she falls back in his
arm dead. He kisses* JESS *and she falls back in the other
arm dead. He faces front as the MUSIC comes UP
again.*) It was just another day. I had found two loves
and lost two loves. The sun set. The city was cold steel
again, like every heart in it. My name is Jack Club.

(*LIGHTS OUT.* MILDRED *and* BRAD *applaud as the
GENERAL LIGHTS come UP again.* JESS *and*
STEPHANIE *have exited through the arch.* WHIT *is
putting his coat on again.*)

MILDRED. Now that was excellent. Exactly right. You
see, Mr. Duckton, everything all of us did is now a
parody. We are anachronisms.

RODNEY. Perhaps. Thank you, Mr. and Mrs. Olive.
Your performances were quite something.

JESS. (*As she enters and crosses to her bag.*) I don't
quite know how to take that.

WHIT. (*Crosses above desk.*) Just take it and be
quiet.

BRAD. I don't agree, however. My style of writing is
still current. I mean, nothing has come along to replace
it yet.

JESS. Oh, we can take that off, too. Come on, Whit,
let's show him. I'm just getting warmed up.

RODNEY. (*Rises.*) No, no, no. This is for me. I'll
show Mr. Benedict what his mystery tales are like if he
wants.

BRAD. I'm not so sure I do want.

RODNEY. It's my turn to twist the knife, as it were.
(*Crosses below desk on way to podium.*) All right, suppose we take one of Mr. Benedict's famous CIA men.
We'll just pick him up in one of your climactic scenes.
(JESS *sits on the sofa and* WHIT *on the settee.*) Come
on, Mr. Benedict, you act it out. Over there. (*Indicates
by desk.*)

BRAD. How will I know what to say? (*Goes by bench.*)

RODNEY. It's my version of your story, so you'll say what I'm thinking.

BRAD. O.K., here goes. (*Sits on the bench as the LIGHTS DIM to the podium light.*)

RODNEY. We find our hero about to stop the take-over of all Allied Missile information by Chaotic. Those are the bad men. The organization always has initials that spell out a name. You've noticed that, haven't you? Mr. Benedict's hero has been looking for the superspy. Superspies always have catchy names, too. We'll call this one "Silver Leg." All through the story, our hero has been having various affairs with various girls in various unusual places like Turkish baths, cemeteries, the subway—but only the express line! Now we find him in his beach-house with his beautiful secretary.

(*LIGHTS DIM on podium and come UP on the desk area. MUSIC of a mod beat accompanies this scene. BRAD is sitting on the bench and his secretary is sitting beside him D. with her feet on his lap. She is dressed in a trench coat and bright-colored boots. She is unusually beautiful and hardly looks like a secretary. When she speaks, it is with a slight foreign accent.*)

SECRETARY. There's something about you, 276390845 —something different.

BRAD. My pajamas are custom-made.

SECRETARY. I've enjoyed this assignment, working for you all day and all night, too.

BRAD. (*Swings her legs away and rises.*) And now the assignment's come to an end.

SECRETARY. (*Seductively.*) No, 276390845, I'm like Contac paper. I'm going to stick around. (*Pulls him to her and plasters herself against him.*)

BRAD. (*Rises again, holding one leg.*) But I've found out who Silver Leg is.

SECRETARY. (*Rises.*) You couldn't have!

BRAD. Yes, I could. (*Pushes her down again.*) I planted one of these. (*Holds up a gold button with a pin on the back.*) It's a honing device and I found out everything. This is a miniature broadcasting station and I've been listening in.

SECRETARY. (*Flings herself full length on the bench.*) No!

BRAD. Yes. I planted it on you and heard you reporting to the agents from Chaotic. I'm sorry, Beauty, but I've got to turn you in.

SECRETARY. (*Rises and comes to him seductively.*) No, not yet.

BRAD. (*Hesitates a moment.*) No, business before pleasure. (*Reaches in his pocket for a revolver.*)

SECRETARY. Wait! There's just one thing I've got to know.

BRAD. Which is?

SECRETARY. Where did you plant the honing device? (*Drops the raincoat and she is dressed in a brief bikini. He looks amused and the LIGHTS BLACKOUT. MUSIC OUT and the room LIGHTS DIM UP to find RODNEY looking front, amused, and the SECRETARY has gone off through the arch.*)

RODNEY. There you are, Mr. Benedict.

JESS. At least she was wearing something—

BRAD. Is that how my books seem?

RODNEY. Your detectives are just as ridiculous as mine if you present them that way. (*Moves to below desk.*)

WHIT. Don't stop, please, Mr. Duckton. Go on.

RODNEY. But that's the end.

WHIT. Where was the honing device planted?

RODNEY. I haven't the faintest idea. I don't write that kind of story. (*Sits on bench.*)

WHIT. Spoilsport.

MILDRED. We seem to have lost our purpose somewhere along the line. If we jab at one another, my dears, we'll never be able to collaborate.

JESS. (*Rises and moves toward* U. L.) What we all need is a drink.

JASON. (*Rises and crosses to her.*) You've run out of your allotted time. The unions, you know. The limousine will arrive in twenty minutes to take you to the airport. . . . (*During the above, a* GRIP *comes in and removes the work light. He comes from* D. L. *and exits the same way.*)

WHIT. This is rather stupid, don't you think? We're supposed to fly down there, spend the night in some dreary little hotel, then clamber into some leaky boat in the afternoon and go off to an island where the house will look exactly like this set. Why don't we just stay here?

JASON. Exteriors. Although the action you write will mostly take place in this room each week, we want you to include some outside shots. Then, there's the press. They will come out Friday morning and take pictures of you in the actual house. Feature stories, you know. Publicity will make the show, not the scripts. (*Realizes the slip he has just made.*) Oh, I didn't mean to say that.

MILDRED. But you did say it.

JASON. I suggest we call this whole thing off and disband until the limousine arrives.

WHIT. Frankly, I don't see that we're going to get any further there than we have here.

JESS. I agree.

BRAD. Maybe we will if we stop making fun of our styles. We each have something individual to contribute and let's concentrate on that.

MILDRED. You're right, young man. (*Rises and crosses to* C.) Come on, let's have that drink together. (*They all start for the arch,* RODNEY *crossing below the desk and* U.)

WHIT. There's a rather festive-looking lounge across the street.

RODNEY. We'll see you in the limousine, Mr. Summers.

JASON. In twenty minutes. (WHIT *and* JESS *gather the glasses and put them into* JESS'S *bag.*) I shall fly down with you and then go straight to Vulture's Vault tonight to make preparations. We wouldn't dream of asking you to take the launch tonight.

MILDRED. Thank goodness. I get seasick enough in the daytime. (*They start talking as they leave.*)

JASON. Wait a minute. (*They all stop.*) Thank the audience.

JESS. (*After a moment, during which they all eye the audience.*) For what, darling?

JASON. For coming.

JESS. We didn't invite them. (*To audience.*) Thank you anyway.

WHIT. Same here.

RODNEY. (*As he and* BRAD *exit through the arch and* R.) They've been remarkably quiet. I should think they'd have been bored to death.

MILDRED. (*As she exits.*) I think they are.

BRAD. (*Off.*) I've just felt embarrassed.

JASON. (*Left alone, he doesn't quite know what to do. He smiles at the audience. He walks down and takes the podium.*) The next scene takes place at Vulture's Vault and I'm sure you'll find it more entertaining. It's got to be. (*Notices the* GRIP *removing the spot in the French windows and then winding up the cable which runs across the stage.*) I really do apologize on behalf of WMT Studios, but at least you got a chance to see how these series start. (*Has picked up the podium and now drops the cards off of it. Now he picks them up.*) I don't know what else to say. Perhaps we'd better have the curtain now. (*There is a pause.*) Oh, dear, I hope the stage manager hasn't left. (*Calls.*) Curtain! (*The curtain starts to close.*) Thank goodness. (*The CUR-TAIN narrowly misses* JASON *and the podium.*)

CURTAIN

SCENE 2

Vulture's Vault. It is the same as the previous scene except now it is real, hence the pipe of lights has been removed out of sight, the tormentors have been put into place. The telephone and electric typewriter remain on the desk and everything else is as it was with the exception of the ash trays being cleaned.

GREGORY, *the butler, is standing directly* C. *behind the curtain. He has his back to the audience. When he does turn, we see he looks remarkably like a Dracula character. He has dark, penetrating eyes, a dark and low widow's peak on his forehead. He speaks in a Middle European accent. He is dressed in formal butler attire. He stands there for a moment and then* JANE, *the maid, comes running down the stairs and right up to him. She is dressed in a maid's uniform and is very pretty and just as dumb as she is pretty.*

GREGORY. (*Without turning to look at her.*) I was calling you, Jane.

JANE. (*Out of breath.*) I heard you. That's why I'm here.

GREGORY. I saw the launch on the horizon. It will be here in three minutes.

JANE. Oh, dear.

GREGORY. What's bothering you?

JANE. The dinner. The recipe Mr. Summers gave me is rather fussy.

GREGORY. I'm sure it will be as delightful as you are, (*Turns to her.*) my dear.

JANE. Thank you, but I'm not used to a gas stove. All the families I worked for on the mainland had electric.

GREGORY. (*Crosses to tray on table above settee. The tray contains a brandy decanter and brandy snifters.*) I have confidence in you, Jane, as does Mr. Summers.

JANE. How do you know what he does if you never saw him till last night?

GREGORY. I have ways of knowing.

JANE. (*Crosses up to him.*) If you ask me, Mr. Summers is going to have a nervous breakdown before this is over.

GREGORY. I know. (*Looks up at ceiling.*) I heard him pacing the floor of his bedroom all night.

JANE. (*Looking up, too.*) When I went in there this morning, his bed hadn't been slept in.

GREGORY. Have you seen him today?

JANE. Haven't laid eyes on him. He said he never eats breakfast but he didn't take lunch, either. Not as much as a cup of coffee. It makes me nervous.

GREGORY. Peculiar. Most peculiar. (*Crosses to French windows.*) Perhaps he is waiting at the dock for the launch. You had better go and check.

JANE. (*Starts to exit through door* U. L.) I got dinner to look after.

GREGORY. There will undoubtedly be a long cocktail hour first. Go to the dock, Jane.

JANE. But my roast is in—

GREGORY. To the dock.

JANE. (*Backs toward arch.*) I don't like going down that steep path.

GREGORY. (*Moves to her.*) You're perfectly safe. It's daylight—now.

JANE. I wouldn't go out there at night. The dark makes me nervous. I always been scared of it.

GREGORY. Jane, the launch will be landing. Go.

JANE. Yes, sir. (*Exits through arch and to* D. R. *almost as if mesmerized.*)

GREGORY. (*Starts to exit through kitchen door, suddenly appears to see the audience. Comes* D. *to* L. *of settee.*) You're not supposed to be here. The authors are arriving to fulfill their commitments, but they don't know what they have committed themselves to. It is for them to find out alone. You disappear now. (*Gestures over their heads in a sweeping arm movement. Looks*

again out front and apparently sees nothing.) Good.
(*Turns and looks at portrait over sofa* L.) We are alone
now. (*Exits through swinging door. After a moment,
from far off, the authors are heard approaching.*)

JESS. (*Off.*) I must say the outside looks like Forest
Lawn.

WHIT. (*Off.*) I hope it has a bar.

RODNEY. (*Off.*) Are you all right, Mildred?

MILDRED. (*Off.*) I'm still queasy from that boat trip.

RODNEY. (*Off.*) That's something I've never been
bothered with—a weak stomach.

MILDRED. (*Off.*) Well, bully for you.

BRAD. (*Off.*) In my books, they would have flown us
over here in a helicopter.

(*They enter through the arch. In spite of themselves,
they are all very excited at being in the actual room
and rush from place to place, examining everything.
BRAD goes to the sofa, JESS to the fireplace to in-
spect the stones, MILDRED to the R. of the desk and
then beside it and searches the drawers, RODNEY
to the French windows, and WHIT stays near the
archway.*)

JESS. Mr. Summers was right. It is exactly the same.

WHIT. Exactly.

MILDRED. Incredible what set designers do, isn't it?

JESS. (*Feels the walls or the stones around the fireplace.*) These are real all right. No canvas.

MILDRED. I can create here. I feel it in my bones.
This just calls for a corpse to be sprawled on it.

BRAD. I go for Danish modern myself. (*Bounces on
sofa.*) This sofa feels like early Salvation Army.

RODNEY. (*Looking out French windows.*) It's a com-
manding view all right. I like this place. I fit right in
here.

JESS. I wouldn't brag. (*Picks up a hideous piece of
objet d'art from table above settee.*) Whit, look. This is
exactly what your Aunt Jennie sent us for a wedding

present. Who would have thought there were two of them?

WHIT. I'm worried about the reception we got. That lovely child met us and then scampered away to the back door. Where is everybody? (*During above,* GREGORY *has rounded the arch from off* L. *and stands directly behind* WHIT. WHIT *turns and looks straight into the evil face.*) Ahhh!

BRAD. You must be Gregory.

GREGORY. That is correct.

BRAD. (*Moves to him.*) Mr. Summers told us you would be here. I am Brad—

GREGORY. I know who you are. I know who you all are.

JESS. And we know who you are, so we're even.

GREGORY. (*Steps into the room.*) What are your wishes?

WHIT. Isn't it cocktail time?

GREGORY. If you wish it to be, sir.

WHIT. I wish it to be desperately.

GREGORY. Then I shall prepare. (JESS *moves* U. *slightly.* BRAD *is standing directly in his way. He stops with his face right against* BRAD.) You will pardon me. (*With a weak smile,* BRAD *stands aside and* GREGORY *walks to the swinging door. The authors are surprised to note a door there, since it is the first time it has been used.*)

JESS. That's a creepy one, isn't it?

RODNEY. (*As* MILDRED *settles in the desk chair.* ROD-NEY *is all enthusiasm.*) The odd servant. Standard of my earlier works. I do hope he's Middle European. It's so beautifully nebulous.

WHIT. (*Crosses to below settee as he looks at portrait* L.) Do you suppose we're going to work with that looking down at us?

MILDRED. I believe that's a rather excellent painting.

RODNEY. (*Moves behind sofa and is about to scratch the painting.*) You can tell by scratching it with your fingernail.

JESS. (*Moves to* WHIT.) I don't think Mr. Summers would approve.

BRAD. (*At French windows.*) It's very barren here. I always thought the tropics were lush with lots of vegetation and palm trees.

JESS. You didn't write "Rain," did you?

WHIT. (*Ambles around the room, now crossing above desk toward closet.*) No, darling, that was Somerset Maugham.

MILDRED. (*Finishing her inspection of the drawers.*) There's nothing here but typing paper.

JESS. What did you expect, dear? A will to be read at midnight? (*Sits on bench.*)

MILDRED. I thought Mr. Summers might have left a note or something.

RODNEY. Strange he didn't meet us at the dock.

WHIT. If he's changing into black tie, I shall spit.

BRAD. He must be around somewhere.

RODNEY. But where?

WHIT. (*Opens the closet door and sees* JASON *standing there. He is dressed in a lighter suit than when we saw him last.*) Here!

RODNEY. Summers. (*He moves to below settee.* JASON *teeters for a moment and then falls face forward to the floor. A knife protrudes from his back. The authors all rush to him,* MILDRED *to* D. R. *below closet,* JESS *and* WHIT *to beside each other,* BRAD *to desk chair. The following four speeches are read together as they move.*)

JESS. What's the matter with him?

BRAD. Catch him!

MILDRED. Look out, he's falling!

WHIT. He's ill. He's unconscious!

(JASON *lies there for a moment. They slowly realize what has happened.*)

JESS. Is he—?

WHIT. He's dead!

MILDRED. (*They are all very quiet and speak just above a whisper.*) A knife in his back.

BRAD. It can't be suicide. (RODNEY *turns and glares at him, then back to body.*)

JESS. (*Tentatively.*) Darling, a real murder.

RODNEY. (*As it slowly hits them all that they are involved in a real murder, he moves in to the desk, staring at* JASON.) Out of a closet, too. That's too perfect to believe.

BRAD. What shall we do?

MILDRED. Call everybody together and expose the murderer.

BRAD. But who is it?

MILDRED. I haven't gotten to that yet.

RODNEY. Oh, dear.

JESS. What is it?

RODNEY. I've never seen a real dead body before. Is that what they look like?

(BRAD *moves in to below desk.*)

WHIT. Evidently.

JESS. Well, one thing is certain.

MILDRED. What?

JESS. We've got the beginning of our plot. Now all we have to do is to solve it.

RODNEY. (*Starts to move* C. *away from* JASON.) Excuse me, please, but I do believe I am going to faint. (*Slowly crumples to the floor as the others stare at him.*)

CURTAIN

ACT TWO

The same. A few minutes later. The body has been re-moved, the small chair and table from below the bookcase have been moved down to in front of the closet door and a scatter rug has been placed over the blood; otherwise, everything is as it was.

RODNEY *is lying on the sofa with his head* U. *He is barely conscious.* JESS *is sitting on the* U. *arm of the sofa with a brandy snifter in her hand.* MIL-DRED *is crossing from* D. C. *to the sofa as the* CUR-TAIN OPENS. GREGORY *is* D. R. *in front of the small table.*

JESS. Try to drink this, Rodney, please. It's a stimulant.

RODNEY. (*Waves it away from his face.*) I know that. I've written these scenes, too, you know.

MILDRED. Have we come into focus yet?

RODNEY. I can see you all quite plainly now.

MILDRED. That's a good sign.

RODNEY. This is the first time I ever fainted.

JESS. Have some more. (*Sips it herself.*)

MILDRED. What did it feel like, Rodney? I always describe it as if the hero feels the room's going round and round and then he falls down a dark tunnel.

RODNEY. (*Matter-of-factly.*) Well, you're wrong. I felt sick and woke up on the floor.

MILDRED. Disappointing, indeed.

JESS. (*Referring to brandy.*) Umm, Five Star. Another brandy, Gregory.

GREGORY. Yes, madame. (*Gets the snifter from* JESS *and pours brandy in it.*)

JESS. Shall we try sitting up now?

RODNEY. You're just like all nurses. I am a me, not a "we." You are not sick and, yes, I shall try sitting up now. (*Sits up.*)

MILDRED. You're just cranky because you're embarrassed. (*Moves behind sofa to help him.*)

RODNEY. Where's Whitney and that Benedict fellow?

JESS. They've taken poor Mr. Summers upstairs. It appears the East Room has a delightful view of the ocean.

MILDRED. (*Ominously.*) Does it have twin beds, dear?

JESS. You're not going to move in, are you?

MILDRED. (*After a quick glance at* GREGORY.) There's bound to be another, you know.

RODNEY. Another murder?

MILDRED. Did you ever write a book with only one corpse?

RODNEY. Good Lord, you're right. At least one in the beginning to get the reader's attention and then another towards the end.

JESS. (*Indicating* GREGORY *to hurry with the brandy.*) Quickly, Gregory.

GREGORY. Yes, madame. (*Comes to her with it.*)

JESS. Just in time, darling. (*Drains it in one swallow. Hands back glass to* GREGORY *who replaces it above settee while* JESS *moves to French windows.*)

MILDRED. (*Comes around sofa and helps* RODNEY *to stand.*) Come on, Rodney, up you get. You can't sit there all evening. There's work to do.

RODNEY. (MILDRED *hauls him up and walks with him, holding his arm. They cross below the desk and to above it very slowly.*) I'm all right now. Silly of me. I do apologize, but the sight of that knife sticking out of Summers' back—

MILDRED. Poppycock! You've used knives dozens of times.

RODNEY. It's one thing to describe a knife protruding between shoulder blades and the blood trickling down his suit, but when you actually see it . . . (*Is*

*now above the desk and gets queasy, causing him to lean
upon the desk.*) Oh, here I go again.

MILDRED. Easy on, Rodney. Think of something
pleasant. (*Helps him to the settee.*)

JESS. Think of the money you're making.

RODNEY. (*As he sits on settee.*) I'm thinking. I'm
thinking.

WHIT. (*As he and* BRAD *come downstairs.* BRAD
moves to above desk.) Where's the brandy? There's
bound to be brandy. There always is.

JESS. Five Star, darling. Gregory.

(GREGORY *pours another brandy.*)

GREGORY. Yes, madame.

BRAD. Summers is lying there very peacefully. He
looks exactly as if— Oh, for God's sake.

MILDRED. What?

BRAD. (*Moves* D. R.) I was going to say, it looks exactly as if he were asleep. I stopped writing lines like
that at N. Y. U.

WHIT. (*Moves to above desk.*) Carrying him upstairs now was very interesting.

JESS. I couldn't be more pleased.

WHIT. Seriously. I always have characters whipping
bodies around as if they were toothpicks. But he was
damned heavy.

MILDRED. Perhaps you're not very strong.

WHIT. I tell you he was a dead weight.

JESS. This is no time for levity. Drink that. (GREGORY
is standing beside WHIT *with the brandy.*)

WHIT. Sorry, darling. (*Drinks the brandy.*)

(GREGORY *returns to above sofa. It is now quite apparent that none of the authors take the tragedy of
the situation seriously. They are always too interested in analyzing what is happening and how it
compares to their writings.*)

RODNEY. He's really dead, isn't he?

BRAD. If you'd carried him upstairs instead of fainting, you'd know he was.

RODNEY. I'm sorry I was unable to help, but—er—

BRAD. Forget it. I'm younger than you are. (*Sits in desk chair.*)

RODNEY. (*Crosses to bench.*) I don't think it's necessary to point that out. (*Gets weak again and sits.*)

MILDRED. (*Moves to above the desk.*) You removed the knife, of course?

WHIT. Yes. (*Quickly finishes the brandy.*)

BRAD. I'm going to remember it. It was like taking a knife out of a wedge of cheese.

JESS. (*Intensely interested, crosses to above desk.*) Camembert or Roquefort?

BRAD. More like Camembert, I think. It just sort of slid out.

(RODNEY *gives a slight shudder and groan.*)

MILDRED. (*Laughs.*) This is going to be something.

JESS. It is something already.

MILDRED. I mean all of our next books. I can't wait until the reviewers notice that we're all using the same line. "The knife came out of his back like we're all using the a wedge of Camembert cheese."

JANE. (*Enters through kitchen door and moves to R. side of settee.*) Excuse me but what shall I do about dinner? (*She is the only one who is visibly upset.*)

WHIT. What did you have in mind?

JANE. Serve it or freeze it?

GREGORY. You're not in the frame of mind to eat right now, are you? (*Starts to exit through kitchen door.*)

RODNEY. No.

(GREGORY *exits,* JANE *starts after him, then suddenly turns and comes below settee.*)

JANE. Isn't anyone going to do anything?

JESS. There's no need to be shrill.

MILDRED. (*They are all very calm except for* JANE.) Do anything about what, dear?

JANE. Mr. Summers.

BRAD. He's in the East Room overlooking the ocean.

JANE. But he's dead—

RODNEY. We know that.

JANE. Murdered. (*Comes* D. C.) Are you all going to sit there?

GREGORY. (*Slips in through the swinging door quickly.*) Jane, you must control yourself.

MILDRED. (*Delighted, she crosses up to* GREGORY.) Very good, Gregory. When the ingenue bursts into hysteria, someone always has to say, "You must control yourself." (*Crosses below him and gets her bag above sofa.*) Do you write?

GREGORY. No, Miss Maxwell.

JANE. I'm sorry. (GREGORY *exits to kitchen.*) But you're all sitting around and doing nothing. Shouldn't someone call the police? (*Crosses above desk, indicating the telephone.*)

RODNEY. (*Turns to others as if* JANE *were an idiot.*) Impossible, isn't it?

MILDRED. (*As* JESS *crosses to the settee.*) Out of the question.

WHIT. You're very naive—Jane, is it?

JANE. Yes. But what's naive about calling the police? Isn't that what they're there for?

BRAD. (*Over-explanatory.*) We can't call them.

JANE. Why not?

RODNEY. (*Rises and moves toward sofa.*) Naturally, the phone is dead.

JANE. You've tried it?

MILDRED. (*With a tolerant smile.*) We don't have to, dear.

JANE. What do you mean?

WHIT. (*Crosses to* JESS.) Perfect line: "What do you mean?" They always say that.

JESS. You amaze me, Whit. You're so perceptive.

JANE. (JESS *sits on settee and* WHIT *on the arm.*)
Pardon me, but how do you know the phone is dead?

RODNEY. Shall we explain it to her?

MILDRED. (*Crosses down to settee and* RODNEY *moves to beside and above her.*) It's very simple, Jane. We are brought out here. We—the great mystery writers of all time. We walk in the door, a body flops out of a closet. Do you really imagine that one of us is going to walk to the phone and call the police on the mainland? Nonsense. (*Sits.*) Of course the phone is dead. It has to be.

JANE. But this isn't a story. This is real.

RODNEY. We're all aware of that, but we're also aware that the phone is dead as a doornail. (*Sits.*)

JANE. I don't believe you. You're all crazy. I'll do it. (*They all watch her tolerantly and with interest as she picks up the phone and jiggles the receiver.*)

JESS. I cherish naivete. It's so rare.

WHIT. You lost it at two and a half.

JESS. And wouldn't you love to know who with.

JANE. (*Into phone.*) Hello . . . hello. . . . The phone is dead.

THE AUTHORS. Uh-huh.

MILDRED. Now that we've wasted ten lines of dialogue, let's get on with it. Any suggestions?

BRAD. I don't suppose any of you has a pencil radio?

RODNEY. I don't even have a pencil.

BRAD. In my books, we'd just take out the pencil, raise the antenna and then talk with the CIA or somebody. (*He has risen.*)

MILDRED. Which might be why your books aren't selling too well any more. (*She continues on with her crocheting.*)

BRAD. Well, they did a helluva lot better than yours did last year.

MILDRED. I'll have you know that—

RODNEY. Please. Please. We must not bicker. (*Pointedly to* BRAD.) We all have respect for one another. Remember?

BRAD. Yes, of course. I'm sorry, Miss Maxwell. I've always bowed to you in your plot lines.

MILDRED. Thank you. And I have always thought that your ingenious devices were marvels—

BRAD. (*Turns to sit in small chair* R.) Thank you.

MILDRED. Fantasies but marvels.

BRAD. (*Sits.*) They do have pencil radios, you know.

MILDRED. Perhaps they do but it's cheating having all those gadgets.

RODNEY. Now that we've ascertained that none of us has a pencil radio or a ray gun or a laser beam and that Mr. Benedict won't self-destruct in five seconds, what are we going to do?

WHIT. (*After a short pause.*) Drink?

JESS. Marvelous idea.

RODNEY. You two certainly do stay in character.

JESS. We try to.

RODNEY. Then I suggest we have some food before you get blotto.

JESS. That sounds a trifle vulgar.

MILDRED. I agree whole-heartedly. Jane, perhaps you could make some small sandwiches. There must be something out there to slap between pieces of bread. Just to tide us over.

JANE. Yes, Miss Maxwell. (*Goes into kitchen.*)

JESS. I hope she's not going to try slapping caviar. Sounds mushy.

WHIT. I think this kitchen is definitely salami.

RODNEY. I don't suppose they have any cottage cheese.

BRAD. (*With a smile as he teases* RODNEY.) Jack Club would eat a raw steak after he took it off his eye.

WHIT. About the cocktails . . .

GREGORY. (*Swings around edge of arch from* U. L.) I shall prepare some cocktails if you wish.

JESS. Gregory, do all butlers eavesdrop?

GREGORY. In your books, madame.

JESS. Touché.

GREGORY. Martinis?

WHIT. Perfect. I have a bottle of Bombay Gin. It's in that initialed leather case with my luggage.

GREGORY. (*Moves to* WHIT.) I have already brought in all the bags and have taken the liberty of placing the Bombay Gin in the pantry. We only have Gilby's.

WHIT. Gregory, you are a true gentleman's gentleman.

GREGORY. Thank you, sir. (*Exits through door* U. L. C. *to kitchen.*)

WHIT. Now that we have taken care of the nourishment situation, what next?

RODNEY. (*Rises.*) Someone has to be in charge. Someone must ask questions and discover clues and things.

MILDRED. Correct.

RODNEY. (*Obviously thinking he is the best one.*) But which of us?

JESS. Whit and I are a team. So we're out.

BRAD. Why not you, Rodney? We'll take it in order of seniority.

RODNEY. (*Crosses to* C. *of desk.*) I wish you wouldn't keep harping on age.

BRAD. I was referring to experience.

RODNEY. (*Pleased.*) Oh. Because, I believe, Miss Maxwell is somewhat older—

MILDRED. What was that, dear?

RODNEY. According to Mystery Writer's Who's Who, you predate me by three months.

MILDRED. That is merely because I lied when my first book came out. I wanted the editors to think I was mature so I said I was twenty when I was only eighteen.

BRAD. (*Rises and crosses to mantelpiece.*) Then it's settled. Rodney, you have the floor.

JESS. (*As* RODNEY *heads for the* D. R. *area.*) That always sounds so stupid. (RODNEY *stops exasperated.*) "You have the floor." What's he supposed to do with it? Polish it?

RODNEY. Mrs. Olive, there is a time and a place for your celebrated wit, but this is neither the time nor the place. If I am in charge, I must have a moment to think. (*Moves* D. R.)

MILDRED. (*Interrupting* RODNEY'S *train of thought again*.) Plunge ahead, that's my motto. If you spend half the day sitting at your typewriter staring out of the window, you get nothing written. I draw the blinds.

RODNEY. Quiet, please. I wish to assess all that has happened and then start the questioning. (*He is* D. R. *and the LIGHTS in the room dim to the SPOT which was the podium light in Act One. As soon as the dim is complete, everyone leaves the stage through the French windows except* RODNEY *who disappears into his own thoughts.*) Obviously none of us did it; therefore, it is either Gregory or Jane. She is too young and naive to be true and he is definitely an odd servant. Odd servants very often are murderers. Now, I'm something of a genius as a mystery writer. I've never fooled myself. There it is. It's a fact. I am a genius. I created Jack Club. If I just act the way he would act then everything will be solved promptly. Now, he would know there is something rotten about those two servants. It's too hard to get domestics these days to have two of them just sitting around on this island. The thing to do is to eavesdrop and find out what they know. (*The room LIGHTS DIM UP with a blue wash. This is the imagination lighting used throughout the act at various times. It must be a different color than the general lighting so the audience knows we are in imagination.*) If I could just get them alone. (*Turns and finds himself alone.*) Good. I got rid of the others. Now to get the odd servant and the naive girl in here. (*Crosses up to arch and turns back.*) Here they come. You can't beat imagination for getting things done quickly. (*Moves to French windows and holds back the* U. *drape.*) I'll just slip behind this. (*Pulls the drape around him and immediately pops his head out the other side.*) Remember, Rodney, you're tough. Like Jack Club. Tough as nails. (*Grimaces and pulls the drape around him.* GREGORY *and* JANE *enter through arch.* GREGORY *is now "The Boss" and uses a different voice and a tougher body.* JANE *is the typical moll of the thirties and talks with a Bronx accent. She chews gum. They come to between the settee and the desk.*)

GREGORY. Good. They took a powder.

JANE. How much time we got?

GREGORY. I can signal now.

JANE. You're a genius, Gregory.

GREGORY. (*Takes a stance.*) I am da Boss.

JANE. Was it tough rubbin' out Summers?

GREGORY. Naw. Just like stickin' a knife in a wedge of Camembert cheese.

JANE. You gonna give it to the others?

GREGORY. If they get in the way, we'll sink them in the ocean in cement galoshes.

JANE. Let's do it anyway, just for practice.

GREGORY. Get the ice first and we'll have fun afterwards.

JANE. Five hundred clams in uncut diamonds, emeralds, and rubies sitting out there in a dinghy.

GREGORY. The biggest heist in history. And they said the crown jools couldn't be stolen. (*Moves* D. C., *his hands in his pockets.*) They reckoned without "Da Boss."

JANE. (*Down to him.*) But you blew it.

GREGORY. (*Twists her arm behind her.*) What do you mean by that?

JANE. Oww, you're hurtin' me.

GREGORY. You only hurt the one you love.

JANE. (*Slowly turns in to him.*) You're aces with me. (*They kiss, a staged "thirties" kiss.*)

GREGORY. How'd I blow it?

JANE. Them writin' people comin' here. You didn't figure that.

GREGORY. No sweat. (*Lets go of her.*) Summers came first and got the Camembert cheese treatment. Now, I'll signal from the tower, the boat comes in and delivers the diamonds. The 'copter is due at midnight and then we'll be off, Hon. (*Clutching her shoulders.*) Anywheres you like. Rio, Capri, Detroit.

JANE. This is it. One big heist and then easy street.

GREGORY. Thirty minutes and they'll be in my mitts. The jools.

JANE. I love the way you say that word. Jools!

GREGORY. Hang loose, Hon. (*Crosses to arch.*) And remember, you're mine. All mine. (*Exits.*)

JANE. (*Moves to R. of settee.*) The jools. That dumb cluck. Little does he know once he gets them, it's curtains for The Boss. That's right. Curtains! (*Flings back the U. drape with a violent gesture and RODNEY is there looking as tough and as much like Jack Club as possible.*)

RODNEY. Hi ya, Baby. (*Moves toward D. C.*)

JANE. Who are you?

RODNEY. (*Takes dime from his pocket and flips it in the air a la George Raft.*) They call me Jack Club! (*Fails to catch the dime and it falls to the floor.*) Damn. (*Reaches down and picks it up. JANE comes down to him.*)

JANE. Jack Club, the Private Eye?

RODNEY. You tagged it, Baby.

JANE. There ain't a hood in the underworld whose chin you ain't scarred and not a hood's dame whose lips you ain't blistered.

RODNEY. So they tell me. (*Puts the dime away and takes out a small pocket nail file and cleans his nails.*)

JANE. How'd you get here?

RODNEY. Swam.

JANE. You're tough, Jack Club. All tough.

RODNEY. So they tell me. Now let's level. The jools is gettin' here in thirty minutes.

JANE. (*Shocked.*) You heard?

RODNEY. (*Puts nail file away and moves R.*) I clean my ears with the barrel of my .22.

JANE. What're you gonna do?

RODNEY. Them jools go back to the Queen of Ilanya and you, Baby—

JANE. Yes.

RODNEY. You go off with me. (*Swaggers up to her.*) You're about to get blistered, Baby. I hope you got Unguentine in your lipstick. (*Grabs her and kisses her violently. She pulls away and slaps his face.*)

JANE. What the hell do you think you're doing?

RODNEY. Kissing you, Baby. Kissing you hard.

JANE. (*Pushes him back.*) Well, just lay off.

RODNEY. You didn't like it?

JANE. You're a dirty old man.

RODNEY. Come on, Baby—

JANE. I'd just as soon kiss a dried sponge.

RODNEY. (*Dropping from character a moment.*) That's not what you're supposed to say. This whole thing is going wrong.

(GREGORY *enters through arch and, unseen by* RODNEY, *crosses to above bench.*)

JANE. The Boss and I get the jools and you get a shiv in the back same as Jason Summers. (*Sees* GREGORY *and now tries to maneuver* RODNEY *into position where* GREGORY *can hit him.*)

RODNEY. So you lured him to his death, eh? (JANE *moves* D. *so* RODNEY *has to come to her.* GREGORY *comes to behind him with the butt of his gun ready to hit* RODNEY *over the head.*) I can see it now. He steps towards you. He puckers up. Then Gregory knifes him.

JANE. Smart, ain't ya? I can't resist ya.

RODNEY. Too smart to fall for that line, Baby. (*Moves away* D. L. *to* JANE *just as* GREGORY *brings the revolver down, missing him.*)

JANE. (D. *to* RODNEY, *turns him.* GREGORY *to behind him.*) You wouldn't give me a kiss even if I begged you?

RODNEY. Not after that bit about the dried sponge.

JANE. (*Seductively, puts her arms around his neck.*) I was only foolin'. Come on, I like antiques.

RODNEY. Since you can't resist, maybe one little

smacker just so you'll have something to remember in stir. (*As he is about to kiss her,* GREGORY *strikes him on the head.* RODNEY *yells and moves* D. C., *hopping from one foot to the other, his hand on his head.*) Oww! That hurts!

GREGORY. It's supposed to.

RODNEY. (*Continues hopping.*) I mean, it really hurts! Oww! Oww!

JANE. Why doesn't he fall down?

GREGORY. He's got a head like a pair of cement galoshes.

RODNEY. (*Below the desk.*) I had no idea it would hurt this much. I always have my heroes hit on the head and they shake it off and go into a fistfight. You know, this really hurts.

JESS. (*Comes downstairs and through arch.*) What is going on down here? Who is yelling like that?

GREGORY. (*Assuming his original character.*) An intruder, Mrs. Olive. I'm afraid I had to resort to violence.

RODNEY. Ow! Ow! Ow!

JESS. Who are you? (*Moves to him.*)

RODNEY. (*Turns to her.*) Jessica, please.

JESS. (*Leans back on desk.*) My God, it's Jack Club. Thank goodness I have Unguentine in my lipstick.

RODNEY. He's the murderer. There. Gregory. And she's his accomplice and my head hurts.

JESS. The servants? No, Mr. Club, the servants never do it any more. That's passé.

RODNEY. (*Getting himself under control.*) OK, see for yourself. I'll prove it to you. Get over there. (*Pushes her* D. R.) This is it, Jane. The showdown. (*Moves in* C.) You take him and the jools or me, Jack Club, without the jools. No woman can resist me. I'm tough. All tough.

GREGORY. (*To the* L. *of* JANE. *He hitches up his pants à la James Cagney.*) OK, Baby, what do ya say?

RODNEY. (*Similar gesture.*) She has no choice, Buddy.

JANE. Give me that. (*Takes the gun from* GREGORY.) Here's my answer, Old Man. (*Points the gun from* GREGORY *to* RODNEY *and fires.* RODNEY *reels into the* D. R. *light as the OTHER LIGHTS in the room dim to out. During the lights-out period,* JANE *and* GREGORY *exit and the others resume their positions as before the imagination.*)

RODNEY. Oh, I'm shot. I'm actually shot. And it hurts. It's not like I thought it would be. I always write "hot lead ripped through his shoulder." But it's worse than that. It just plain hurts. (*Steps back and sits in small chair* R.) How can I expect my characters to carry on after something like this? They ought to go to hospitals for weeks and then get workmen's compensation. (*Recovers himself into reality.*) I never thought it would be like that, but I guess it must be. I always thought of myself as a realistic author but this head-hitting and getting shot twice a book isn't an easy matter at all. No, I'm definitely not for reality. (*Room LIGHTS DIM UP.*) There's only one thing for me to do now that I'm faced with a real murder. (*Rises and assumes position* D. R. *he was in when he began imagining.*) And that's to shut up!

MILDRED. (*After a pause while they all watch* RODNEY.) How much longer do we have to wait for you to assess all that has happened?

RODNEY. (*Moves to above desk chair.*) I have come to a conclusion. I have nothing to say at all except that the butler did it.

JESS. (*Laughs.*) The butler?

WHIT. Gregory? That's too obvious, Old Man.

RODNEY. Don't call me "old man."

WHIT. I wasn't referring to your age. It was a term of endearment. Don't be so sensitive.

BRAD. In my books, there weren't any butlers. They're from a different era.

RODNEY. (*As* GREGORY *enters from kitchen with a tray containing six martini glasses and a pitcher of martinis.*) Mark my words, the butler did it.

GREGORY. Cocktails are ready.

WHIT. (*Takes the tray.*) Thank you, Gregory. It appears the only thing he did was to make drinks.

RODNEY. (*Above desk chair.*) I wouldn't drink one of those.

JESS. I would and will.

RODNEY. Better have him take a swallow first.

WHIT. Nonsense, you've got a Roman Emperor complex.

MILDRED. Still, Rodney may have a point.

WHIT. Would you mind, Gregory?

GREGORY. Not at all, sir. I don't like to drink on duty, but since you have requested it. (*He drinks and RODNEY·sits at desk.*)

WHIT. Not too dry?

GREGORY. Perfection, sir. (*Puts glass on tray.*)

WHIT. Thank you, Gregory. I shall serve them.

GREGORY. Thank you, sir. (*Exits into kitchen.*)

WHIT. (*As he serves them to JESS, MILDRED, and BRAD. RODNEY refuses.*) Are you satisfied, Rodney?

RODNEY. It must be a slow-acting poison. Wait a minute.

JESS. Then we'd hear a gurgling gasp, wouldn't we?

WHIT. Gurgling gasp. Alliteration. I like that.

MILDRED. What do you suppose a gurgling gasp sounds like?

(WHIT *has just gotten back to* RODNEY *who refuses a drink. From behind the kitchen door comes a gurgling gasp and the sound of a body hitting the floor.*)

RODNEY. (*With extreme conceit.*) Exactly like that, I should imagine.

(JESS *rises*, BRAD *moves* D.)

MILDRED. Anyone want to go take a look?

RODNEY. I'm not budging from this spot. I don't react well to dead bodies.

JESS. (*Moves* R. *to* WHIT.) Whit, go and see if Gregory's tossed off the mortal coil. (*Puts drink on tray.*)

WHIT. I can't. I'd spill this tray of martinis.

BRAD. (*Puts glass back and exits* U. L.) Then it's up to me. I have a strong stomach.

MILDRED. If the butler's passed over, Rodney, it sort of knocks your theory into a cocked hat, doesn't it?

RODNEY. Perhaps he drank the martini, knowing it was poisoned but realizing he was caught.

MILDRED. Twaddle.

JESS. I loathe bad language.

WHIT. (*Looking at tray he is holding.*) I wish Brad would hurry up. I'm dying for one of these but not if they're lethal.

BRAD. (*Enters and comes* L.) He's dead, all right.

MILDRED. Well, now, things are bustling, aren't they? Two down and five to go.

BRAD. The poor guy looks terrible. All twisted up like a pretzel.

RODNEY. When I have someone poisoned, I always say he grasps his throat and falls over dead.

BRAD. It must have been agonizing. Want to have a look?

JESS. You'd better not. We're running low on brandy.

WHIT. Jess, smell this glass he drank out of.

MILDRED. (*As* BRAD *sits on sofa.*) If the murderer has any sense at all, it will be odorless. That's what I always use.

JESS. (*After she smells glass.*) Whew, it's worse than moonshine.

WHIT. Now, smell the others.

BRAD. What will that prove?

WHIT. Whether just one martini was poisoned or all of them.

JESS. (*Having sniffed them.*) They smell all right.

WHIT. Good. (*Puts down tray on desk.*) Then we can drink them.

RODNEY. Have you no compassion at all? Summers and now Gregory dead.

WHIT. That's the past, old boy. It's the future I'm thinking about and I can see a drink in mine. (*Hands one to* JESS *and takes one for himself.*) Here. Cheers. (*They drink.*)

MILDRED. (*Rises and crosses to below settee.*) Then if only one of the drinks was poisoned, it mustn't have mattered who got it. I mean, the murderer didn't seem to care which of us drank it.

BRAD. It couldn't be one of us. We were here all the time.

WHIT. We're all suspect. Have we kept a strict eye on each other?

JESS. Of course, darling.

WHIT. Wrong. When we carried poor Summers upstairs, Brad and I both washed up afterwards. Separately, of course. Jess rushed out to get brandy when Rodney collapsed, Mildred went to the ladies' while we were waiting for Rodney to "take over" the questioning. There we are.

RODNEY. Obviously I am exonerated.

WHIT. No. You were hovering by the tray when Gregory brought it in. You could have slipped something in it.

RODNEY. For that matter, so could you.

WHIT. Well, now that you bring it up, yes.

BRAD. So any of us could either have slipped something in the drink or perhaps the glass before the drink was mixed.

JESS. (*Happily.*) Isn't it marvelous? We're all still in the running. (*Sits on the bench.*)

MILDRED. Did you expect anything else? It's too soon to find out the guilty party.

BRAD. What about the maid?

JESS. Jane? Hadn't we better tell her?

RODNEY. She'll find out soon enough.

JESS. How?

(*There is a scream from* JANE *from off* L.)

RODNEY. Like that. She was bound to stumble over him sooner or later.

JANE. (*Comes rushing on quite shaken.*) Help . . . something terrible—

THE AUTHORS. —has happened!

MILDRED. (*Moves to* JANE.) That's a trite line, dear.

BRAD. We all know Gregory is dead.

JANE. He's just lying there in the pantry.

MILDRED. And you're properly hysterical. Good girl. Come along, now, I'll make you a nice cup of tea.

JANE. Mr. Summers and now Gregory.

MILDRED. (*As she puts her arm around* JANE *and takes her off* U. L.) No need to sum it up yet, dear. We can add. (*To the others.*) You carry on. I'll be right back. (*As they go through the door.*) Now, pick up your feet, dear. You stumbled over him once already. That's right. Take a giant step.

BRAD. (*Rises and crosses up to door.*) Mildred's quite calm about this, isn't she?

RODNEY. Now don't start pitting us against one another. Those are such boring scenes.

BRAD. Then if there's someone else on this island, we ought to set out and find him.

JESS. Or her. (*Takes tray and moves it to table above sofa.*) Always say "him or her." Never narrow down the field until you're certain.

BRAD. Let's search the island.

RODNEY. Useless.

BRAD. Why?

RODNEY. (*As* JESS *sits on settee.*) It always is. If you'd paid attention to the older genre of mysteries like Mildred's and mine, you'd know we're alone here.

BRAD. But hadn't we better make sure?

WHIT. I suppose you're right.

BRAD. (*Moves to* C.) We'll all go off in different directions and scour the place.

RODNEY. (*Rises wearily.*) It won't take long.

BRAD. (*In the arch.*) I'll go this way. Whitney, you that way. Rodney, towards the north and Jess take the upstairs.

JESS. Good. I don't want to scrape my heels on the rocks. These are I. Miller shoes.

BRAD. Ready. Go.

MILDRED. (*As they are about to exit through arch, she enters.*) Stop! Where are you off to?

RODNEY. This young fellow thinks we should search the island.

MILDRED. Waste of time. Naturally, we're all alone here.

RODNEY. I know that. The Olives know that. You know that, but he doesn't know it.

MILDRED. Then we'll prove it to him. Where do I go?

BRAD. You take the wine cellar.

WHIT. I'll trade with you.

BRAD. I am giving out the assignments. Ready and go. (*They start to exit with* BRAD *going* U. R. *and* D., RODNEY *through arch and to dining room,* JESS *upstairs,* WHIT *through French windows, and* MILDRED *through kitchen door.*)

RODNEY. Which way is north again?

BRAD. That way.

MILDRED. I wish someone would move this body.

(JESS *starts upstairs and as soon as the others are off, she comes down and looks around the room, picks up a martini.* WHIT *comes back in through French windows and to behind her.*)

WHIT. Caught you!

JESS. (*Gives a small squeal.*) Whitney Olive, don't you ever do that to me again.

WHIT. I knew you'd come right back here like a homing pigeon.

JESS. What about you?

WHIT. (*Takes a drink.*) I hate solitary alcoholics.

JESS. (*Sits on settee.*) All this searching business is

ridiculous, but we do have to humor the younger generation.

WHIT. (*After he sits beside her.*) That's a really
well-mixed martini. Too bad he died.

JESS. Whit, I feel terribly guilty.

WHIT. Look here, you didn't do it, did you?

JESS. Of course not, but here we are right up to our
collective necks in two murders and I'm not as nervous
as I should be.

WHIT. That's because we're used to it.

JESS. But only in an imaginary sort of way.

WHIT. This whole thing doesn't seem real somehow.

JESS. Why don't we just solve it and then get on with
our writing? We're not going to meet a deadline with
bodies lying about the corridors and not knowing who
did it.

WHIT. Do you suppose we could solve it?

JESS. But, darling, of course. We've solved every
murder we've ever been involved with.

WHIT. Because we decided who the murderer was
before the crime was committed. This time we're not
working backwards.

JESS. (*Rises and circles above settee.*) It might be
fun starting from the top. Now, we know it isn't any
of us. I mean, a mystery writer committing murder
would be dirty pool, wouldn't it?

WHIT. (*To table above settee.*) Dishonorable dis-
charge from the mystery writers' guild.

JESS. (*Glass down on table.*) Then it must be Jane.

WHIT. She's awfully pretty.

JESS. (*To R. of settee.*) Do you remember "The Case
of the Two-Legged Secretary"?

WHIT. Intimately.

JESS. It was your idea to have the pretty girl the
murderess and it went into a second printing two weeks
after publication. (*Moves to below desk.*)

WHIT. You're right.

JESS. I usually am.

WHIT. You're conceited, too.

JESS. (*Moves* D. R.) Then, if it is Jane, what would we do if we were writing it?

WHIT. (*Joins* JESS D. R.) Have her discovered committing another murder?

JESS. No, we'd have her make some idiotic slip and then the beautiful and brilliant wife, the part we created after me, would say something like, "Aha! You slipped up that time!"

(*LIGHTS on the room dim to the* D. R. *spotlight.*)

WHIT. I'd rewrite that line, but go on.

JESS. So all we have to do is to get this Jane to make a stupid mistake.

WHIT. But how?

JESS. You're half of this writing team. Give me a little help.

WHIT. I'm trying. (*From off kitchen, they hear the sound of* JANE *sobbing.*)

JESS. Here she comes now. Be nonchalant. (*They rush back to the sofa and sit. To be nonchalant,* JESS *is leaning against the arm, her legs crossed.* WHIT *is posing dramatically. Imaginary LIGHTS come up on room.*)

JANE. (*Enters from kitchen carrying small plate of sandwiches. She is sobbing and crosses to the* R. *of the settee. In this imaginary scene,* JANE *is as innocent-seeming as possible.*) You look so nonchalant.

JESS. Thank you, darling.

JANE. I wish I could be that calm but every time I come out of the pantry I have to step over Gregory.

JESS. You're working under a great handicap but the sandwiches do look delicious. (*Takes one as does* WHIT.)

WHIT. Salami?

JESS. (*Smells one.*) Salami.

JANE. (*Puts plate on table above settee.*) Where's everyone else?

WHIT. Searching the island.

JANE. They will not find anyone on Vulture's Vault. Gregory and I have been here for two days and we never saw a sign of a soul.

JESS. You were here alone?

WHIT. Together?

JANE. Yes.

JESS. (*Casually bites sandwich.*) Were you lovers?

JANE. Of course not. What a thing to say.

WHIT. (*To* JESS.) You're letting your imagination run away with you.

JESS. We always have a bit of sex in our books, don't we?

WHIT. (*To* JANE.) How well did you know Gregory?

JANE. We never met until we got on the launch to come here. (*Moves* R.) You see, I've been out of a job because I've been ill. Up until last January, I worked for Mrs. Plato Onderdonk.

JESS. (*A knowing look to* WHIT.) We've never met her.

JANE. (*Getting carried away with her innocent act.*) A truly kind woman. She paid for all my hospital bills.

JESS. Did she take you with her between houses, New York and Newport?

JANE. Oh, yes, indeed.

JESS. And out on the yacht?

JANE. Oh, yes, indeed.

JESS. Aha! (*Rises and puts glass on table.*) You slipped up that time.

JANE. Oh, no!

WHIT. I said I was going to rewrite that line.

JESS. Don't you see, Whit?

WHIT. See what?

JESS. Mrs. Plato Onderdonk doesn't own a yacht. She gets seasick in her bathtub. That was your mistake, Jane. You've revealed your true self.

JANE. (*Breaks down in violent weeping.*) All right, I did it. I killed them both.

WHIT. (*To* JESS.) You did it, darling. You're a marvel.

JESS. Thank you, darling.

WHIT. (*Turns and looks at* JANE *who has frozen in her weeping position.*) What's the matter with her?

JESS. We've stopped imagining we're writing this, so she's stopped, too.

WHIT. Are we going to leave her like that?

JESS. Well, it's the end of the story. Close the book. (*Sits on settee.*)

WHIT. But this isn't how it would turn out if she really did commit those two murders.

JESS. Probably not.

WHIT. (*After a pause during which he thinks. Alarmed.*) Jess!

JESS. (*Startled.*) What, Whit? Whit, what? What— Oh, the hell with it.

WHIT. Jess, she would do something desperate, wouldn't she?

JANE. (*Comes out of freeze and pulls revolver from her uniform pocket. She now speaks in a deeper, tougher voice.*) You're damned right she would.

JESS. Oh, I don't like this at all.

JANE. You stupid fools. Of course I'll do something desperate. I'll kill the two of you.

JESS. No, you mustn't kill the authors. That's shooting the hand that types you.

WHIT. I agree wholeheartedly.

JANE. You first, Mr. Olive. (*Points gun at him.*) If you have anything to say, say it fast.

WHIT. Could I have another martini?

JANE. Here it comes.

JESS. (*Rises and runs into* D. R. *area.*) Stop! Stop it, both of you! I'm writing half of this and I say, stop it! (*They freeze with* WHIT's *hands over his eyes and* JANE *about to shoot.*) That's better. Whitney, come over here. (*He joins her as the LIGHTS DIM to* D. R. *spot.* JANE *exits through kitchen door.*) What went wrong?

WHIT. We finished the story all right, but there were a few extra pages.

JESS. Do you suppose that would happen at the end of all our books if they were real?

WHIT. Possibly.

JESS. I've definitely decided I don't approve of or take any delight in real murders at all.

WHIT. Let's go back to our martinis and shut up. (*SPOT DIMS and room LIGHTS UP.*)

JESS. Good idea. (*They tiptoe back to the settee, get their drinks and sit.*) We were right about one thing, though.

WHIT. I'd like to know what.

JESS. Jane must be the murderer. There's no one else it could be.

WHIT: Much too obvious, dear. There's got to be a plot twist somewhere.

RODNEY. (*Enters through arch and from* L. *He is brushing himself off.*) Stupid waste of time. There's nothing to be discovered out there. Not even a decent rock formation.

JESS. Never mind, Rodney, we've made the impetuous young author happy.

MILDRED. (*Enters from kitchen, something in her hand behind her back.*) Merry Christmas.

WHIT. My calendar watch must have stopped.

MILDRED. Guess what I found in the wine cellar?

WHIT. What?

MILDRED. (*Holds up a very dusty old bottle of wine.*) Wine.

RODNEY. That's hardly surprising.

MILDRED. It looks older than your original horror story.

JESS. And much more tasty. Don't just stand there, Mildred, open it and we'll have a toast.

MILDRED. (*As she exits.*) To anything in particular?

JESS. Our partnership. I think we've come up with some marvelous plot points already.

RODNEY. (*Comes* D. *to bench and sits.*) You're rather

cold-blooded, you know. I suppose you'd like us to bury both of them together and have a double tombstone reading, "Here lie two plot points."

BRAD. (*Enters through arch.*) Anyone find anything?

JESS. Mildred discovered a marvelous, decaying bottle of aged wine.

BRAD. (*Comes to between settee and desk.*) I must apologize to all of you. You were right. The island is deserted.

JESS. Live and learn.

WHIT. Now, if everyone will listen to me for a moment, I suggest we call in Jane and give her the third degree. You know, under a bare bulb while we sit around chewing gum and cracking nuts.

(MILDRED *reenters from kitchen. She has uncorked the bottle.*)

JESS. Because if it isn't Jane, then it's one of us.

RODNEY. Impossible.

MILDRED. (*By* L. *of settee after putting bottle on table.*) Rodney, you have been consistently wrong ever since this evening started.

RODNEY. You think it's one of us?

MILDRED. It has to be. I just found Jane with her head sticking in the oven and the gas turned on.

RODNEY. Dead?

MILDRED. She wasn't baking an apricot upside-down cake.

BRAD. Good God.

WHIT. That's a stupid line, Brad. Say something more pertinent.

JESS. Did you turn off the gas?

WHIT. (*As* MILDRED *nods.*) Now, that's pertinent.

MILDRED. (*Moves* D. *by sofa.*) It seems to me it's time we solved these crimes. Before you know it, we'll be dead. That's what always happens in those books by that woman—Agatha something-or-other.

RODNEY. Christie.

MILDRED. Yes, that's her. Why don't we take her theories and start from there? The guilty person is always the least likely one. Who's that? Why, the one who is done away with first. He's only pretending.

WHIT. That's old hat. Done to death. I even saw a play where it was used. "Any Number Can Die" by Fred Carmichael.

RODNEY. Never heard of him.

BRAD. (*To* MILDRED.) That theory doesn't hold water. Summers is dead all right. Whit and I carried him upstairs and we know.

WHIT. Agreed.

MILDRED. (*Sits on sofa and resumes her work.*) So much for Agatha Christian.

JESS. Christie, darling, Christie.

MILDRED. She'll never last.

JESS. Of course it could be one of us.

BRAD. How?

JESS. We all spent the night in that dreary hotel on the mainland. (*Rises and crosses to French windows.*) Anyone could have rented or stolen a launch, put-putted over here, killed Summers, gone back again, and showed up for breakfast. (*Turns back to room.*) A squirt of Murine in the eyes and who would know?

MILDRED. That's true.

JESS. Except Whit or me, of course. (*Crosses to* WHIT *and puts her arm around him.*) We're married and sleep together, unusual as it may seem these days.

WHIT. But either of us could have given the other a sleeping pill and done it.

JESS. You and your big mouth.

BRAD. (*Moves* D.) Now that you've found we're all potentially guilty, what next?

RODNEY. Maybe if we all say what's on our minds, we'll hit on something.

WHIT. My mind's on—

MILDRED. We know. Another drink.

WHIT. Brilliant deduction, my dear Maxwell. (*Hands his glass to* JESS *who refills it.*)

RODNEY. (*Rises and goes to* BRAD.) What about you, Benedict? We don't know what you're thinking.

BRAD. Well, I—it's just that—

RODNEY. Come on. Speak up.

BRAD. (*Crosses below desk.*) If I were to say what's on my mind, I'm sure no one would agree. I've been trained to think in a different era of time than you have. (*Room LIGHTS DIM to SPOT area* D. R. *He crosses into it.*) If I were like my heroes with their electronic equipment, I'd go back to just before we all went to search the island, before Jane was killed. (*Takes button like he used before from under his lapel.*) This innocent-looking thing is a honing device. I'd have hidden one on each person and then, with this innocent-seeming pen, I could have listened in to any conversation they might have had. (*Holds up ball-point pen.*) That's what I'd have done . . . then, when they went to search . . . (*Imagination LIGHT wash comes up and they are all in same positions as they were before the search began.*) Ready and go.

(*They all turn to go and it is seen that all of them have the gold button honing devices pinned in the middle of their backs. In the long speech of* BRAD'S JESS *and* WHIT *have gotten theirs from the back of the sofa,* JESS *has pinned one on* RODNEY, *and* MILDRED *put one on her last time offstage.*)

RODNEY. (*Turns back to* BRAD.) Which way is north again?

BRAD. That way.

MILDRED. (*As she exits to kitchen as before.*) I wish someone would move this body.

BRAD. (*After they have completed exits as before.*) Now to use this innocent-seeming device. (*Takes out pen. Each click of it brings in another station.*)

ANNOUNCER. ". . . for that peppy feeling, use Bloodpep every morning. It's time to stop being dead."

BRAD. Wrong channel. (*Clicks pen again.*)

JANE. (*Over microphone.*) . . . I thought I'd never get you alone.

BRAD. That's Jane's voice.

JANE. (*Over microphone.*) I've got the plans, but we'd better not be seen talking out here. Even those stupid authors might suspect something.

BRAD. Who's she talking to?

JANE. (*Over microphone.*) Meet me in the living room. I've got the plans hidden away in a book . . . no, not here. Save the romance for later. . . . Oh, all right, if you insist. . . . (*Sound of a very noisy kiss.*)

BRAD. Those spies are all the same. (*Puts pen away.*) The living room? That's here. I'd better conceal myself and find out who the Master Spy is. (*He ducks down D. of the desk.*)

JANE. (*Comes from kitchen, looks around. Takes book from bookcase U. R., brings it down to desk. Calls.*) Come on, hurry up before the others get back.

(*Footsteps are heard coming to door from kitchen.*)

RODNEY. (*Enters.*) Where are the plans? (*In this imagination sequence, RODNEY is a smooth but hard villain and JANE a rather sexy agent.*)

JANE. Keep your shirt on. I'm getting them. (*Takes paper out of book. These are the plans and they are actually on flash paper which can be obtained at any magic supply shop.*)

RODNEY. (*Crosses D. to her.*) Chaotic will pay millions for those. Millions.

JANE. (*Holding up the plans.*) Here they are.

RODNEY. Perfect. (*Reaches for them, but she holds them back.*) Every missile site on the eastern seaboard. How did you get them?

JANE. The usual way. No one can resist my body.

RODNEY. The *entire* eastern seaboard?

JANE. In six days. I was slowed down in Jacksonville.

RODNEY. Incredible.

JANE. (*Waving paper in front of him.*) Now I want what's coming to me.

RODNEY. And that's just what you're going to get. (*Takes pocket comb from his pocket.*)

JANE. I want the dough. This is no time to fix your hair with that innocent-seeming comb.

RODNEY. Your usefulness is over, my dear. (*Slides his fingers along the comb while pointing it at her. The teeth of the comb click and she stiffens and collapses. He grabs her, tries to put plans back in book, but can't get near the desk with the weight of the body.*) Now the plans are all mine. But what to do with you? I know. The oven. Those stupid authors will never suspect that Chaotic is mixed up in this. They're too concerned with themselves. (*Has been dragging her off through the kitchen door.*)

BRAD. (*Comes out of hiding.*) So that's it. (*Pulls out pen and clicks it.*) Now to listen what he's doing with the poor child.

RODNEY. (*Over microphone.*) Good lord, she's heavy.

BRAD. He's getting old.

RODNEY. (*Over microphone.*) I'm not getting old. Just tired. Now, down you go. Open comes the oven door. (*SOUND of metal door opening.*) And on goes the gas. (*SOUND of hissing.*)

BRAD. Now for the showdown. The way I write it, I get the plans back and capture Rodney Duckton, Master Spy. Reality isn't so different from imagination, after all. (*Puts pen away.*)

RODNEY. (*Enters from kitchen smoking a cigarette. He dusts off his clothes.*) Now to condense these plans into a microdot on film. (*Sees BRAD.*) Oh—did you—did you find anything in your search of the island? (*Puts the plans behind his back.*)

BRAD. Never mind the act, Rodney. Give me the plans.

RODNEY. Of course, Brad Benedict. (*Takes comb from his pocket.*) As soon as I comb my hair. (*Puts plans on desk.*)

BRAD. Don't pull that innocent-seeming comb on me.
See this! (*Takes a cigarette lighter from his pocket.*)

RODNEY. I know about the innocent-seeming cigarette
lighter. I can stop you fast enough. (*Holds up his wrist
and points the watch toward* BRAD.)

BRAD. (*In terror, holds his hands up.*) Not the innocent-seeming wristwatch?

RODNEY. That's right, Brother. (*Picks up plans.*)

BRAD. So you win, but you won't keep the plans.

RODNEY. Of course I will. They're right here and
they're mine. All mine. (*The cigarette inadvertently
touches the plans and the flash paper disappears in a
flash.*) Good lord.

BRAD. When they touch a Chaotic agent, they self-
destruct in five seconds.

RODNEY. I should have known. (*Collapses on desk
with his head on it as he sits on bench.*) I killed Summers, Gregory, and Jane to get those and now my plans
have all gone up in smoke. (*Raises his head to see
BRAD's shoe on the desk in front of him. BRAD is about
to tie his shoelace.*) .What are you doing?

BRAD. Just tying my shoelace.

RODNEY. (*Rises.*) You think that innocent-seeming
shoelace will stop this innocent-seeming wristwatch, do
you? (*Points watch at him.*)

BRAD. That's what it's made for.

RODNEY Then take this. (*His hand on his tie clasp.*)

BRAD. The innocent-seeming tie clasp. (RODNEY *flicks
it,* BRAD *stiffens and reels into* D. R. *area.*) This is
wrong. All wrong. Chaotic isn't supposed to win.

RODNEY. (*Backs away holding the book from desk.
The room LIGHTS dim to out and BRAD is left in the
D. R. spot.*) You didn't write this, Brother. This is reality. (*He puts the book back in the bookcase and resumes
original positions as the others do.*)

BRAD. Oh, Bradley Bruce Benedict, it isn't a good
idea to say what's on your mind. Of course, Rodney
may be the murderer. He's old and senile and his mind
may have snapped. Now stop it! Every time someone

thinks he knows who the murderer is, that person gets killed. I'll just say nothing.

(*General room LIGHTS up and all are in positions as before* BRAD'S *imagination.*)

MILDRED. Mr. Benedict . . . Brad—

BRAD. (*Coming to.*) Oh, sorry. My mind was wandering.

MILDRED. You were just telling us that if you said what was on your mind, we wouldn't agree. Just what is on your mind?

BRAD. Nothing. Not a thing.

MILDRED. Just as I thought.

BRAD. However, I can make a prediction.

JESS. Well, go ahead. Make it.

BRAD. Rodney, you're going to be killed next.

RODNEY. That's not a very polite thing to say.

BRAD. (*Moves to bookcase.*) Nevertheless, it follows the pattern.

RODNEY. (*To* BRAD.) What pattern?

BRAD. I'd rather not say.

JESS. If you know something and you're not telling us, then you're cheating. We're supposed to be collaborating.

BRAD. (*Takes book from bookcase.*) Oh, here's the first book I ever wrote.

RODNEY. (*Standing beside him.*) This is no time for narcissism. Why did you say I was going to be killed next?

BRAD. Because you are. (*Opens book and a puff of smoke comes out. He grabs his throat and falls to the floor. The effect can be gotten by cutting the pages out of the center of the book and putting some flour or Fuller's Earth in there with a small rubber syringe-bulb which* BRAD *merely presses.*)

MILDRED. (*After they look at him for a moment.*) Everyone is wrong about everything tonight.

RODNEY. Thank God for that.

JESS. (JESS *and* WHIT *cross to the body,* MILDRED *comes over and picks up the book.*) He's dead, of course. (*They all turn and glare at her.*) Ask a silly question, get a silly answer.

MILDRED. (*Examining book.*) A poison gas capsule set to a spring in this cut-out book. Ingenious. The murderer knew that was a foolproof way of getting Brad.

RODNEY. (*As* MILDRED *replaces book in bookcase.*) Why? Any of us could have opened that.

MILDRED. Not that book, Honey. It was Brad's first. Remember "Lightning Cube"?

RODNEY. Oh, God, yes. It was awful.

WHIT. He improved after that.

MILDRED. The murderer knew that none of us would dream of opening that book except Brad. And, of course, he couldn't resist it.

RODNEY. Marvelous, Mildred. Your famed deductive mind works even when you're not writing the story. Keep going.

MILDRED. I can't think properly with that body messing up the living room. Since there are only two gentlemen left, I suggest they remove Mr. Benedict.

RODNEY. (*As he gets* BRAD *by his shoulders and* WHIT, *by his feet.*) Where to?

MILDRED. How do I know? With the others?

RODNEY. (*They lift* BRAD. *Start for kitchen.*) Jane is in the kitchen. (*Head for the stairs.*) Summers is upstairs. (*Head for kitchen again.*) Gregory is in the pantry. We'll put him in there. It's closer. (*They go off through swinging door.*)

MILDRED. (*As* JESS *sits on the settee.*) Now things are getting exciting.

JESS. I must admit to feeling a trifle nervous.

MILDRED. (*Crosses above to* R. *side of settee.*) Rot. We're getting down to the nitty-gritty of the whole business. This is when I shine.

JESS. I'd just as soon we figured it out in some comfortable lounge on the mainland.

MILDRED. (*As* RODNEY *and* WHIT *reenter.*) We'd

only have to come back. Return to the scene of the crime and all that.

JESS. Well, I, for one, want to leave Vulture's Vault.

RODNEY. (*As they move to above desk.*) I, for two, agree with you. How do we go about it?

JESS. In those movies where a plane crashes on a deserted island, they always write a tremendous "help!" in the sand.

RODNEY. Excellent suggestion.

JESS. There's only one thing wrong with it.

RODNEY. What?

JESS. No sand. This island is completely rock.

WHIT. Then we'll build a fire.

MILDRED. Out of rocks? Weren't you ever a Boy Scout?

WHIT. No, they ripped off my badge when they found my canteen full of martinis. (JESS *giggles.*)

MILDRED. There is a time when humor is unwelcome, Mr. Olive, and this is one of those times.

RODNEY. The furniture!

JESS. I assume that's a non-sequitur, Rodney, but you did succeed in changing the subject.

RODNEY. We'll burn the furniture. The smoke will bring help and then we'll write this whole thing up for the TV show. (*Picks up the small chair* R. *and crosses toward French windows with it.*) I'll take this chair. Jess, have you got any matches?

JESS. Yes.

RODNEY. Whitney, do you think you can manage that table?

WHIT. (*Picks up table and starts out with it.*) I've been under ones that are smaller, but I'll try.

MILDRED. (*Rises.*) I must tell you that I have very little faith in this scheme.

JESS. (*Rises.*) Me, too.

RODNEY. (*As he goes out French windows.*) What's wrong with it?

MILDRED. It's too simple. (*Follows* RODNEY *off.*)

JESS. Far, far too simple. If this would work, then

everyone would have done it in all our books. (*Picks up bag.*)

WHIT. Maybe we never thought to have them think of it. (*Follows.*)

JESS. I'll answer that when I've figured it out. (*Exits.*)

RODNEY. (*Off.*) Now pile them on top of each other.

WHIT. (*Off.*) This table feels like it's made of stone. Do you suppose it will burn?

JESS. (*Off.*) If the fire gets going, I'll look in the larder for some marshmallows.

RODNEY. (*A yell from him and then he rushes in with his hand to his neck.*) Ow! Get away! Stop that! Damn thing!

JESS. (*Off.*) What's the matter?

RODNEY. A bee stung me.

MILDRED. (*Rushes in to him.*) Where? Let me see.

JESS. (*Off.*) I'll make some mud. That's the best thing.

RODNEY. (*Removes his hand. To* MILDRED.) Here.

MILDRED. (*Ominously.*) Oh, dear.

RODNEY. It's bad, isn't it?

MILDRED. (*Walks away.*) Very.

WHIT. (*Comes in and drags* RODNEY *out.*) Rodney, come along. Jessica has made some beautiful mud. If you don't use it, she'll only put it on her face.

RODNEY. It hurts.

WHIT. Of course it does, Rodney, but you're a brave boy. (*They are off.*)

MILDRED. Good-bye, Rodney Duckton. You were one of my favorite authors. Bee sting indeed! (*Crosses to desk.*) I used that one in "The Case of the South American Headhunter." I know a blowgun dart when I see one. Dipped in curare no doubt. They always are. Aha, the unusual weapon. This is right up my line. Mildred, my girl, go to it. (*Crosses to below desk.*) Now for the surprise ending. The murderer is not Jessica as she was helping Rodney with the chair. It's not Whitney as he was piling the table on top of the chair. Therefore, by

process of elimination, the murderer is me! (*Happily.*)
How's that for a surprise ending? (*Does a take.*) No,
I didn't do it. I know that. (*Crosses* D. R. *as SPOT-
LIGHT comes up. Room lights dim.*) Then, if it isn't
me, it must be one of those Olives. Intriguing idea, you
know. Just like I'd construct it. Down to three people
and one of them is guilty. How would I conclude it?
The Olives would come in and announce, all surprised-
like, that Rodney is dead from a blowgun. Yes, that's
how it would begin. . . . (*Room LIGHTS come up in
the imagination wash.*)

WHIT. (*As he and* JESS *rush in to in front of settee.*) Mildred. It's Rodney—

MILDRED. (*Playing it all innocent.*) What about him?

JESS. He's dead.

WHIT. It wasn't a bee sting. It was a dart from a
blowgun.

JESS. The kind of murder you would commit.

MILDRED. (*In mock surprise, sits on desk chair.*)
Well, what do you know?

JESS. (*As she and* WHIT *surround* MILDRED.) Con-
fess, Mildred. Then the three of us will sit down and
write the story before you give yourself up.

WHIT. The royalties will be astounding.

JESS. We'll see that your next of kin gets your share.

MILDRED. How generous of you, but you've forgotten
one thing.

WHIT. That line again?

MILDRED. Yes, you've forgotten that I know I didn't
do it; therefore, it must be you.

WHIT AND JESS. (*After a look to each other.*) We
forgot about that.

MILDRED. I thought you'd reckoned without my deductive mind.

WHIT AND JESS. How true.

MILDRED. But why did you do it?

WHIT. Surely you can figure that out.

JESS. We're dried up. No new idea in ages. Our books
are getting pedantic—

WHIT. Sloppy—

JESS. (*Crosses around desk and sits on bench.*) Predictable. The only way they'll sell is to get rid of the competition.

WHIT. (*Sits on top of desk.*) So we're ridding the world of all mystery writers, one by one.

JESS. We're quite insane.

WHIT. Utterly, completely mad.

MILDRED. I should have guessed. Now, there's only one thing left to do, isn't there?

JESS AND WHIT. What?

MILDRED. Kill me, of course. No, I didn't say that. You didn't hear me. Tell me you didn't hear me.

JESS AND WHIT. We heard you. (JESS *opens purse and takes out small blowgun which is actually a lipstick.* WHIT *takes a small blowgun from his pocket.*)

MILDRED. Me and my big mouth.

JESS. (*As* WHIT *rises.*) Put that down, Whitney. It's my turn. (*Rises and kneels on the bench.*)

WHIT. (*Like a schoolboy.*) It is not.

JESS. Is so.

WHIT. Is not.

MILDRED. (*Rises and crosses to* C.) Why don't you two figure it out while I go upstairs and freshen up?

JESS AND WHIT. Stay where you are. (JESS *moves to* MILDRED'S L. *and* WHIT *to her* R.)

JESS. All right, darling, let's do it together.

WHIT. Agreed. On the count of three. One—two— three— (JESS *puffs on the lipstick and* WHIT *on the blowgun.* MILDRED *ducks. They obviously hit each other.* WHIT, *with a hand to his neck.*) Jessica!

JESS. Whitney! (*Similar gesture to her neck. They both do identical circles and fall to the floor.*)

MILDRED. (*Goes to* D. R. *spot area.* JESS *and* WHIT *go out through French windows during her speech.*) There, that's a surprise ending. But it won't work in real life, will it? It's stupid and silly and I'd rip it out of my typewriter and start over. The truth is, no one can predict reality and I'll just have to wait and find out like one of my readers does. They must be about to come back saying— (*LIGHTS in room come back up again.*)

WHIT. (*Comes in as before with* JESS.) Mildred, it's Rodney—

MILDRED. What about him?

JESS. He's dead.

WHIT. It wasn't a bee sting. It was a—

MILDRED. Dart from a blowgun, I know.

JESS. (*Toward* MILDRED, *front of bench.*) Of course you knew. It's your kind of murder.

MILDRED. It may be the kind of murder I'd think up, dear, but not the kind I'd commit. No, I'm not the murdering type.

JESS. Neither are we.

MILDRED. One of you must be. Or both. I was thinking just now and—

WHIT. And?

MILDRED. (*Rises and crosses to* JESS.) Nothing. It's just that I had an idea— (*Grabs* JESS' *bag.*)

JESS. Give me that.

MILDRED. After I search it.

WHIT. (D. *to* JESS' L.) Let her have it, darling. She can't use your Master Charge here.

JESS. (*As* MILDRED *turns to desk and goes through purse.*) I knew she was a murderer but I had no idea she was a purse-snatcher.

MILDRED. (*Taking out lipstick which* JESS *used in the dream as a blowgun.*) Aha, just as I thought.

JESS. It's not your shade.

MILDRED. Think you can fool an old hand like me, dear? Take that. (*She blows through the end of the lipstick.* WHIT *and* JESS *exchange looks.*)

WHIT. She's completely crackers.

JESS. If you're hungry, there's food in the kitchen.

MILDRED. It's just a lipstick.

JESS. Surprise! Surprise!

MILDRED. (*As* JESS *takes lipstick and returns it to bag.*) Then how did you do it? Where's the blowgun?

JESS. (*Sits on settee.*) We might ask you the same question.

WHIT. (*Crosses to* JESS.) Yes, how did you do it?

MILDRED. Me?

WHIT. If it wasn't either of us, it's got to be you. (*Sits.*)

MILDRED. Either of you? Why not both of you?

JESS. You honestly think we'd go around killing people? Why don't you go away somewhere?

MILDRED. (*Sits on bench.*) Oh, no, I'm not falling for that line. I'm staying right here where I can keep an eye on you.

WHIT. And we're staying right here where we can do ditto.

JESS. (*After a pause during which they stare at each other.*) How long before one starves to death?

WHIT. I'd die of thirst long before.

MILDRED. (*Rises and crosses above desk.*) I, for one, am not going to waste time. There's money to be made out of this situation and I'm going to get it. I'll break into magazines with this one. (*Sits at desk chair and puts paper in typewriter.*) Serial rights and then movie rights. My biggest moneymaker. I think I'll call it "A Night of Horror."

JESS. It isn't over yet.

WHIT. (*To* JESS.) Is she going to finish it in jail?

MILDRED. (*Has tried to type.*) Damn typewriter doesn't work.

JESS. You are old-fashioned, Mildred. It's electric.

MILDRED. Oh, hank you. Where's the button? Ah. (*Turns it on. It hums. She is about to type.*)

WHIT. Go ahead. Don't let us disturb you.

MILDRED. (*Raises finger, then stops and looks at them.*) You seem a little overanxious for me to start. Of course. Ingenious!

JESS. What now?

MILDRED. Electricity. The typewriter is rigged to electrocute me.

WHIT. (*At the end of his patience.*) Well, really!

MILDRED. (*Rises.*) You thought I'd fall for that? With the ingenious murders I write?

JESS. (*Rises and moves above desk.*) This has gone too far. Even if we were guilty, we'd never think up anything as stupid as that.

MILDRED. Stupid, dear? One of my best murders was the electric heater in the bathtub.

JESS. Here, I'll type for you. (*Stands by typewriter as MILDRED fades.*) Whit, darling?

WHIT. Yes, dear.

JESS. By some odd chance, you didn't rig this, did you?

WHIT. Jessica!

JESS. Just asking. (*Types.*) M-a-r-t-i-n-i. There, Mildred. (*Returns to settee and sits.*) It's all yours.

MILDRED. (*Sits at typewriter.*) Well, it was a good idea.

JESS. Use it sometime.

MILDRED. (*Typing.*) "A Night of Horror" by Mildred Z. (*As she hits the "Z," there is a bright flash of light, the LIGHTS in the room flicker on and off quickly. Possibly there is a flash from the typewriter if it can be arranged. MILDRED screams, stands, does a circle and falls to the floor above the desk.*)

WHIT. (*After he and JESS rise and cross to the body.*) It was rigged.

JESS. Is she dead?

WHIT. Everyone else is, she must be. Dead as a doornail. I always hated that line.

JESS. (*Crosses to typewriter.*) The murderer knew it would kill her. No one else would type the letter "Z."

WHIT. (*JESS goes to body and he leans over desk to typewriter.*) She short-circuited the typewriter, too.

JESS. At least she went out writing. That's rather poetic justice.

WHIT. Oh, my God!

JESS. What's the matter, darling?

WHIT. Then it's you.

JESS. I was thinking the same thing about you.

WHIT. Why did you do it?

JESS. I didn't.

WHIT. You must have. I didn't.

JESS. Of course you did. There's no one else but me and I didn't do it. (*Starts to cry.*)

WHIT. (*Crosses to her.*) You're suffering pangs of remorse. That's good for you.

JESS. (*Sits on settee.*) I am not crying because of any pangs.

WHIT. Then why?

JESS. Because this is the first time you've ever kept anything from me.

WHIT. (*Sits beside her.*) I haven't kept a thing from you.

JESS. What do you call six murders? Nothing? Our whole marriage is over. It was based on trust and understanding and mutual faith and now you have lied to me.

WHIT. I could say the same thing about you.

JESS. No, you couldn't. I'm innocent.

WHIT. So am I.

JESS. I don't believe you.

WHIT. Look at me. Look at this face. (*Takes her face in his hands and turns it to him.*)

JESS. I always liked that face—even the peculiar parts of it.

WHIT. What peculiar parts?

JESS. Well, your nose isn't what it should be and one eye is different from the other.

WHIT. I like that. Here I've never complained about you all these years through every one of your hair colors.

JESS. I was only trying to please you.

WHIT. You've always known when I was lying. Now, look at me. I didn't commit those beastly murders.

JESS. (*Suddenly very happy.*) I believe you. Oh, Whit, darling, I believe you.

WHIT. Now, tell me something.

JESS. What?

WHIT. Why did you commit them?

JESS. (*Starts crying again.*) I didn't. I didn't. I swear on our next royalty check.

WHIT. Honestly?

JESS. Cross my heart and hope to . . . (*Looks up toward Heaven.*) No, I take it back. I didn't say that.

WHIT. Then, if we didn't do it and there's no one else here except dead people, we've finally come upon the perfect crime.

JESS. I always said it could be committed.

WHIT. We should celebrate.

JESS. The wine. (*Points to opened bottle* MILDRED *had brought in.*)

WHIT. Excellent. (*Rises and goes to it.*) I hope it's a good year.

JESS. (*Blows her nose with handkerchief from bag.*) I do feel rather a fool having suspected you, darling.

WHIT. Think nothing of it. I suspected you. (*Pours wine into glasses set above settee.*)

JESS. What are we going to do now? Sit here drinking until the launch comes?

WHIT. We'll be delightfully tipsy.

JESS. How can I keep a happy outlook on our work after tonight?

WHIT. (*Sits and gives her glass.*) This might help.

JESS. It's bound to.

WHIT. (*As they raise their glasses in a toast.*) To our greatest mystery—yet to come. (*They drink.*)

JESS. (*With a grimace.*) Oh, this wasn't a good year at all.

WHIT. It wasn't even a good month.

JESS. Do you think it was made from grapes or onions?

WHIT. Bitter and acrid, that's what it tastes like. Where have I heard that before?

JESS. You wrote it in "The Poisoned Corpse." Remember?

WHIT. That's right. The wine was bitter and acrid.

(*They slowly turn to each other as the truth dawns on them.*) Jess.

JESS. Whit.

WHIT. The murderer knew we'd drink this.

JESS. Damn!

WHIT. Don't be upset, darling. We're going together. (*Neither of them is really horribly upset by what has happened and they take it quite calmly.*)

JESS. It's not that, but we don't know who did it.

WHIT. That is rather upsetting.

JESS. It's like turning the last page of a mystery book and having it say, "Guess who?"

WHIT. (*Yawns as the poison takes effect.*) Perhaps we'll find out in the great library in the sky.

JESS. (*Yawns.*) Do you think they'll have all our books?

WHIT. Bound in gold leaf.

JESS. And we'll pick up the *Times* and be at the top of the best seller lists every Sunday morning.

WHIT. (*As they grow more tired, he takes her hand.*) Heavenly.

JESS. Exactly.

WHIT. But I can't wait. I want to know who it is now.

JESS. So do I, darling.

(*SOUND of front door opening off through arch. A LIGHT streams in and FOOTSTEPS are heard.*)

WHIT. What's that?

JESS. Someone's coming in. Oh, Whit, we're going to get our last wish. We'll see who it is.

WHIT. I'm too tired to turn my head.

JESS. (*Calls weakly through a yawn.*) Will you stop dragging your feet and hurry up?

(*There is a small, cackling laugh and* JASON SUMMERS *comes through the arch. He is in a different suit than the one in which he was murdered.*)

JASON. Here I am. (*Steps over* MILDRED *and comes to settee.*)

JESS. Jason Summers!

WHIT. What a bore!

JASON. Don't you like it?

JESS. It's been done to death. The first one killed is the murderer.

WHIT. I'm sure you were dead when we carried you upstairs.

JASON. I was.

JESS. I loathe science fiction.

JASON. Jason Summers was dead. But I am Grady Summers.

WHIT. This is even worse. His twin brother, I assume?

JASON. That's correct.

JESS. Dirty pool! Oh, such dirty pool!

JASON. After you two are gone, I shall have done it— the perfect crime.

WHIT. But why?

JASON. (*Crosses* D. L.) My brother, Jason, always had everything. I had nothing.

WHIT. Oh, I abhor speeches like this.

JESS. Explanatory and they're always long and boring.

JASON. (*Moves to* L. *of settee.*) Hear me out. When Jason told me of his plan to bring you here and how he'd come up with the greatest murder script in history . . .

WHIT. I know. You wanted to do him one better—

JESS. And so you committed real murders—

JASON. How did you know?

WHIT. We write these things.

JESS. We used to write them. Whit, I can't take any long speech from him. (*Settles down on* WHIT's *shoulder.*) I'm going right now.

JASON. But it's my right to say something. Every murderer gets to tell how he did it, step by step.

WHIT. Not this time, old boy. (JASON *tries to inter-*

rupt.) Sorry to leave you, but that's the way the ball bounces. (*His head goes down against* JESS'.)

JASON. (*Crosses above settee.*) But I have so much to say. (WHIT *and* JESS *yawn together and die.*) My murders. (*Moves to* R. *of settee.*) I have made history tonight. I have committed the ultimate in crime. (*Above settee to* U. C.) This is the perfect mystery.

MILDRED. (*Rises up from floor. She speaks calmly.*) Oh, I don't think so.

JESS. (*As she and* WHIT *sit up.*) It doesn't have any punch at the end.

WHIT. Rewrite. It needs a tremendous rewrite.

JASON. (*Now himself again.*) I think it's excellent.

MILDRED. No, no, no. You don't know anything about it. Mr. Summers, we are the experts. (*To arch and calls.*) Come back in now.

JASON. (*Moves to bench and sits.*) The suspense is terrific.

WHIT. But the characters aren't any good.

JESS. You can't combine all those styles into one coherent work.

(BRAD *enters through kitchen door and* RODNEY *through the arch.*)

BRAD. (*Sits on sofa.*) I heard everything offstage.

RODNEY. If we could bring Jack Club in after the first murder . . .

MILDRED. Jack Club is out. He was good in his time, but—

BRAD. Perhaps if we made him a man from the CIA—

RODNEY. People are tired of that. (*Crosses* D. R. *and addresses the audience directly.*) Aren't you?

JESS. (*Crosses to* RODNEY.) Rodney, darling, they still think we're on the island.

RODNEY. (*To audience.*) You don't, do you?

JESS. Of course they do. We told them we were moving from the studio to the island and we closed the curtain and opened it up again and they naturally thought we *were* on the island.

RODNEY. Just because we said so?

JESS. Of course.

RODNEY. (*To audience.*) What a fabulous group you are. A trifle gullible, but fabulous.

(GREGORY *and* JANE *enter from the kitchen. They both talk quite naturally now. He has his shirt off and a makeup towel around his neck. Most of his heavy makeup has been removed.*)

GREGORY. If we work any longer, we'll have to get overtime. The Union says—

JASON. I am well aware of the Union. (*Sits at desk, takes checkbook from drawer.*) I'll write you out a check immediately.

JANE. (*As* MILDRED *crosses to sofa and sits, she and* GREGORY *move to desk.*) I hope you were pleased with our work.

JESS. (*Moves to her bag by the settee and sits.*) You were marvelous, darling.

JANE. When you get the script finished, can we audition for the parts?

WHIT. Of course.

JASON. (*Writing checks.*) We won't pay above scale.

GREGORY. I'll have to talk to my agent.

RODNEY. (*Crosses to* JESS *at settee.*) We don't want to keep the audience here any longer, do we?

JESS. Heavens, no. They'd be bored to death with the rewrites.

RODNEY. (*Comes* D. C. *to the audience.*) Thank you all very much for coming. Your reactions have been a big help. You see, before we came here tonight, we all met at that restaurant across the way and decided this would be the best thing to do—pretend we were really on the island. Even Jason Summers liked the idea and he did turn in a reasonably good performance.

JASON. (*Modestly.*) I used to do a little community theater work.

WHIT. Do you think we've given them their money's worth?

JESS. Of course, darling. Eight murders. What did they expect—World War Three?

MILDRED. (*Rises and speaks to audience.*) So go home now and don't worry about a thing. Murder is all in books and stories. It can't happen here.

(*There is a loud scream from the back of the theater aisle.*)

JASON. (*They all rise and look toward the sound.*) What's that? (*Moves* D. L. *looking.*)

RODNEY. It came from over there.

BRAD. (*As they all come* D.) It's a woman.

JESS. Another improvisation?

MILDRED. Sounded real to me.

(*The following depends upon the actual theater the play is being presented in. Either the box office girl or an usher or someone else recognizable to the audience comes down the aisle and is helped up onto the stage by* JASON *and* BRAD. *She is gasping for breath.*)

JASON. What is it? What's happening?

JESS. It's that girl from the box office.

BRAD. She's ill.

MILDRED. Nonsense. She's dying.

RODNEY. Murder?

BOX OFFICE GIRL. (*Is now being held between* JASON *and* BRAD.) It's—it's— (*They all ad-lib.*)

JASON. (*Shouting them down.*) Be quiet! Shut up! Let her speak!

BOX OFFICE GIRL. Poison—in the refreshments—poison—

WHIT. I'm glad we stayed backstage at intermission.

JASON. Quiet!

BOX OFFICE GIRL. I know who did it. (*She is hanging over* JASON'S *arm.*)

JASON. Who was it?

BOX OFFICE GIRL. It was—it was—

JASON. Yes. Yes.

BOX OFFICE GIRL. It was . . . it was

JESS. (*Puts her hand over the* GIRL'S *mouth and turns to the others.*) Don't you dare say another word.

JASON. What are you doing?

JESS. Don't let her give away the ending. This is a real crime. This is our script. All we have to do is figure out who did it.

(JASON *lowers the* GIRL *to the ground, and the others all start talking together, forming small groups, ignoring the* GIRL *completely. The following speeches are together.*)

RODNEY. If Jack Club were here, he'd look for a beautiful woman.

BRAD. (*Joining* RODNEY.) I wonder if she has any secret plans on her.

MILDRED. (*Joining them* C.) Poison is always useful, but what kind? Something rare, I hope.

JESS. (*To* WHIT.) We'd best have martini and discuss this.

WHIT. We've got to get a second murder from somewhere.

JANE. (*To* GREGORY.) This isn't in my contract.

GREGORY. We're going into overtime.

(*They all continue jabbering away as*)

THE CURTAIN FALLS

PROPERTY PLOT

ACT ONE

Scene One

PRESET:
　Work light on stand D. L.
　Package of cigarettes and matches on desk
　Electric typewriter on desk
　Liquor bottle in desk drawer
　Strip of spots hanging down on pipe

Off Right:
　Tote bag with thermos of martinis, three glasses, small bottle
　　of olives, small fork, compact, cigarette lighter (JESS)
　Bag with crocheting (MILDRED)
　Speaker's podium (JASON)
　Six file cards (JASON)
　Lit cigarette in cigarette holder (GEORGE)
　Plane ticket (GEORGE)
　Sling (GEORGE)
　Sunglasses (GEORGE)
　Large, stuffed envelope (GEORGE)
　Small radio (GRIP)
　Revolver with blanks (GEORGE)
　Placards reading "WILL YOU BE MINE?", "NO!",
　　"THEN THIS SHALL BE YOUR FATE!", and
　　"SCREAM!" (GRIP)
　Revolver (JESS)
　Gold button with pin on back (BRAD)
　Large white envelope containing small slips of paper (GRIP)

Off Left:
　Cigarette lighter (WHIT)

Scene Two

PRESET:
　Raise strip of spots on pipe
　Clean ashtrays

ACT TWO

PRESET:
　Brandy decanter, 3 snifters, 2 wine glasses on tray above
　　settee

MILDRED'S bag above sofa
Dime in pocket (RODNEY)
Nail file in pocket (RODNEY)
Gold painted pin under lapel (BRAD)
Gold painted pins, 3 of them, stuck above settee
Ball-point pen in pocket (BRAD)
Flash paper plans in book in bookcase
Pocket comb in pocket (RODNEY)
Wristwatch on RODNEY
Cigarette lighter in pocket (BRAD)
Tie clasp (RODNEY)
Copy of "Lightning Cube" with cut-out pages and white
    powder in it in rubber syringe in bookcase
Lipstick in JESS'S purse
Blowgun in WHIT'S pocket
Handkerchief in JESS'S bag
Checkbook and pen in desk drawer

Off Right:
Revolver (GREGORY)

Off Left:
Revolver (JANE)
Tray with pitcher of martinis and 6 glasses filled with martinis
    (GREGORY)
Small plate of sandwiches (JANE)
Dusty, old wine bottle (MILDRED)
Gold painted button with pin (MILDRED)
Lit cigarette (RODNEY)
Makeup towel (GREGORY)

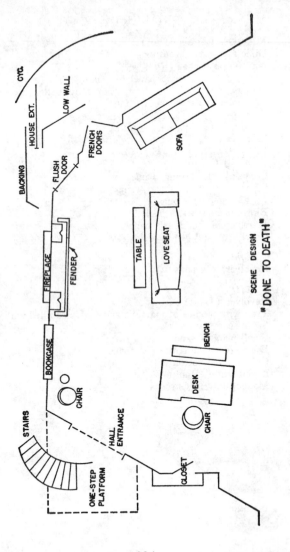

SCENE DESIGN
"DONE TO DEATH"

CYC.

HOUSE EXT.

LOW WALL

BACKING

FLUSH DOOR

FRENCH DOORS

SOFA

FIREPLACE

FENDER

TABLE

LOVE SEAT

BOOKCASE

CHAIR

BENCH

DESK

CHAIR

STAIRS

ONE-STEP PLATFORM

HALL ENTRANCE

CLOSET

104